POINT CRiME

# THE EAST END MURDERS

## Brotherly Love



**Anne Cassidy**

SCHOLASTIC

*Have you read...?*

**The East End Murders 1:**
A Family Affair
End of the Line

**The East End Murders 2:**
No Through Road
Accidental Death

*Look out for...*

**The East End Murders 4:**
Death by Drowning



Scholastic Children's Books,
Commonwealth House, 1–19 New Oxford Street,
London WC1A 1NU, UK
a division of Scholastic Ltd
London ~ New York ~ Toronto ~ Sydney ~ Auckland
Mexico City ~ New Delhi ~ Hong Kong

First published in the UK by Scholastic Ltd, 1997
This edition published by Scholastic Ltd, 1999



ISBN 0 439 01056 X



Typeset by TW Typesetting, Midsomer Norton, Somerset
Printed by Cox and Wyman Ltd, Reading, Berks.

10 9 8 7 6 5 4 3 2 1

# Contents

# 1

# Fireworks

Jack Ross was stabbed to death on Bonfire Night. He was outside the gates of Wood Road Park with his girlfriend Louise Palmer when he was attacked. The street was empty because all the kids and adults were at the local fireworks display. I was even there with my friend Billy Rogers and like everyone else I had my neck craned to look at the explosions of colour from the giant fireworks that glittered and sparkled in the black sky.

Some people said it was a gang fight. Others said it was a robbery that went wrong. I heard that the knife was small and sleek and the blade flicked out so smoothly and silently that Jack Ross hardly felt it go into his chest. It was ten centimetres long and it broke into a main artery. He fell on the ground, his girlfriend crouching down, her knees rubbing on the raw paving stones, her arms around her boyfriend's limp body.

I didn't see the stabbing, didn't even know that it had happened until much later when the wail of the police sirens cut across the whizzing and popping of the fireworks. Momentarily distracted, the kids had turned away from the display and run off in pairs and groups towards the park exit in the direction of the police cars.

All the while, I found out afterwards, Jack Ross had been lying on the pavement. The knife a few metres away, up-ended in the gutter. His girlfriend, Louise, on the ground beside him, rocking back and forth, whispering something in her dead boyfriend's ear.

Earlier that evening Billy and I had passed by the sign that said *Wood Road Park Grand Firework Display.* We had to pay at the gate and Billy rolled his eyes getting the money out.

"Surely we've got something better to do than watch a load of fireworks going up in smoke!" he said, grumpily.

"It's for a good cause," I said.

We were in the middle of a crowd of about four hundred people on the field at the far end of the park. It was an unseasonably mild autumn night and I had a new leather jacket on that I'd just bought. Billy was beside me as we walked by the food stalls that had been set up along the edge. Each one had a sign: *Indian Snacks*, *Chinese Noodles*, *Hot Dogs* and *Hamburgers*. A low growl was forming in my stomach.

"I'm hungry," I said. "Fancy a samosa?"

"Nah," Billy said, his voice low, uninterested.

I got my money out and saw that Miss Eliot, a teacher I knew from my old school, was serving food.

"There you are, Patsy," she said, wrapping up the hot samosas. "I hear you're working as a private eye these days."

I didn't answer. I could tell by the mild sarcasm in her voice that it wasn't a serious question. In the eighteen months since I'd left school I'd met a number of people who were surprised at what I'd chosen to do for a living.

I took the samosas and said, "It's a tough job but somebody's got to do it!"

"What happened to university?" she said, pleasantly.

It was a loaded question and I was struggling to answer it when a bang that sounded like an atomic bomb went off on the main field. I turned round to look at a kaleidoscope of colour in the sky, the crowd around me making an "ooing" sound every time the design changed. A few metres away from me was Billy, his shoulders slouched, his head barely tilted to look at the display.

"I'll see you later," I said to Miss Eliot and she raised her eyebrows significantly, as if she thought I was trying to avoid her question. I ignored her and walked back to Billy.

"Are you going to the car auctions this week?" I said, my voice light, chatty.

"Might do," he said, walking along with me, "fancy coming?"

"I said I might see Brian," I started. Brian was this kid I'd been seeing on and off since the summer. Billy's face dropped and he turned away.

"But it wasn't definite," I said. "I could come if you wanted me to."

"Where's lover-boy tonight?" Billy said in a light voice, as if he didn't really care what the answer was.

"He's working late," I said, casually. The truth was I hadn't felt like seeing him that evening. Although we'd had a nice time when we first started seeing each other I was becoming increasingly fed up. I'd put him off and told him I'd see him at the weekend.

I felt irritated with myself. It would have been nice, like old times, for me and Billy to go to the car auctions. To spend a few hours on a Saturday afternoon wandering among the lines of cars, looking at the tyres and the paintwork, sitting in the front seats, touching all the switches and turning the steering wheels. It would have been a good thing for Billy to buy a wrecked car that he could spend hours working on. Maybe it would have helped him forget his recent experiences.

"I'm not sure what I'm doing on Saturday, anyway," Billy said. "I might be going out with some mates."

I was cross with myself for not being more positive. I was about to speak when I noticed his hand reaching inside his jacket and pulling out a packet of cigarettes. He picked one out and stuck it lazily in his mouth and began to pat his pockets, looking for his lighter.

"I thought you were giving them up!" I said.

"Maybe," he said, pulling a lighter out that was the shape of a lipstick. With a click the flame appeared and he fed it to the cigarette and inhaled deeply. "There's Perry and his mates. I want a word with him," he said and walked off. I watched him go with a sinking heart.

Billy and I had been best friends for years. Once or twice we'd pushed things a bit further and found we liked each other in a different and interesting way. Romance had always scared us both off, though, and we'd ended up pulling back to the starting line, beginning again, pretending that nothing had happened and that we were just a couple of mates.

He walked across the field and stood by a group of young men with shaved heads. One of them slapped him on the back and appeared to laugh loudly. I could see Billy smiling and getting his cigarettes out and offering them round.

I pursed my lips with dismay. He had recently become friendly with a new crowd. They had skin-head haircuts and earrings and didn't seem to be able to string more than a few words together.

Don't get me wrong, I'm not prejudiced but I couldn't help feeling protective about my oldest friend. It was only a couple of months since he'd been accused of a crime and put into prison. It had only been for fourteen days, but Billy had said that it seemed like fourteen years. Since then he'd been difficult, lethargic, uninterested in work and friends. He'd taken to smoking, one cigarette after another, until his clothes and his house smelt of nicotine. He'd taken to enjoying the company of kids who'd left school when they felt like it and who seemed to spend their days hanging around the shopping centres and their nights in questionable pubs.

I was worried about him.

The crack of a Catherine wheel made me jump and I looked across to the main display to see frantic swirls of pink and blue light against the night sky. There were dozens of kids milling around me going back and forth into the crowd, watching the display for a minute and then backing out and running off towards groups of friends over by the food or drink stalls.

The closeness of the crowds and the surrounding smoke from the display was making me feel hot and

I unzipped my new leather jacket to let some air in. I stroked the soft leather and felt a thrill of pleasure.

It had taken weeks for me to buy it. Not to save the money up, I don't mean that, but just to make the decision that it was right for me. It wasn't anything special, just black with a zip front; there were loads of them on market stalls everywhere. I'd been wearing it with a long chiffon scarf loosely tagged round my neck. *It looks great*, Billy had said when I took it out of the bag and put it on. *You look like a biker chick*, he'd said laughing and pretending to rev up a motor bike. I'd told him not to be silly, but I'd been secretly pleased. For a few moments he'd seemed like the old Billy. I hadn't yet shown the jacket to Brian.

A rocket shot up into the sky and gave a thin piercing cry before it exploded into what looked like a thousand fragments of light. Around it I noticed a faint drizzle blurring the colours and realized that it had started to rain. A few umbrellas popped up among the crowd and more and more groups of school kids seemed to fall back from the main display, bored perhaps, fed up with the pyrotechnics, more interested in their own little friendship groups. I began to shuffle around, wondering whether to make my way home. I'd lost sight of Billy and realized that among all the faces I couldn't see one that looked familiar. I was on the brink of getting depressed, so I decided to have a look around for Billy and then go home.

The sirens started then. The sounds seemed to criss-cross with the popping and banging and ooing that was coming from the display. They were in the background at first, away in the distance, the kind of sound that punctuates the night air in every big city. They were persistent, though, and came closer. There were two or three sirens, I thought idly, putting my hand up to my hair to feel the rain getting heavier.

Then the word seemed to spread around me. *There's been a stabbing*, a voice said, then another, louder, full of excitement, *A STABBING!* It changed then to *someone's got stabbed* and *some kids have been stabbed*. Like Chinese whispers the words jumped from one group of young people to another. Some adults holding very small children looked around in a puzzled way at the exodus in the direction of the police sirens, their blue lights visible then across the field.

I found myself following, leaving the fireworks behind and half walking, half running across the field, my DMs slipping and sliding here and there where the well-trodden ground had become slippery under the rain.

I looked around for a moment to see if Billy was there but I was swept quickly along by the crowd who were elbowing past me. Several adults were beginning to leave the fireworks and follow the crowd of kids; my old teacher, Miss Eliot, was among them.

We crammed out of one of the park exits and round the bend of the road. A couple of police cars were parked at angles, their red lights blinking on and off. Miss Eliot had pushed her way up to the front and was talking to a policeman, her hand cupped behind her ear, as if she couldn't hear what was being said. An ambulance screeched to a halt some metres away and two paramedics jumped out and walked quickly towards the main park gates.

Then Miss Eliot was shouting at me: "Patsy, come up here and help me." A policeman held the way open for me and I edged forward. By then, several other adults had got through the crowds and were talking to the police, looking cagily over towards the park gate at a young man lying on the ground.

I found myself looking. All I could see was the girl kneeling across him and a paramedic with his ear on the young man's chest.

"The police want us to make a cordon. So that the children can't see what's happening!" Miss Eliot shouted. "Patsy, you go over there." She directed me towards the ornate railings that ran up to the park gate.

I walked gingerly across and found myself standing side by side with a young WPC. I couldn't help but look back over my shoulder at the kid who was lying on the ground. He was lit up by a yellow security light that was above the park gates. I could see everything and it wasn't nice. The paramedic was shaking his head and the girl was sitting cross-legged, with her head in her hands. The dead boy was lying on his back, his jacket hanging open, his arm lying on the pavement. I looked away. The rain was teaming down and I felt my hair wet and clingy on my face.

I didn't want to look back but something was niggling me.

A rocket went off with a bang from the field behind the school, as the firework display reached its finale. It was followed by what sounded like a dozen more, one after the other, launched into the sky, giving a dazzling display of noise and colour that momentarily pulled the crowd's attention away.

That was when I looked back at the dead boy. The paramedic was just about to lay a plastic sheet over him. The leather jacket was lying open, dipping on to the pavement. It was black and had a zip up the front.

He was wearing the same leather jacket as me.

Except that he wouldn't be wearing it any more.

# 2
# Friends

The ambulance left just before eleven. I found Billy on the field amid the damp fireworks and the straggling crowds. There were policemen and women dotted about, talking and taking notes from what was left of the audience, many looking shocked, upset even. There were also others who looked secretly thrilled as though they had come for one sort of entertainment and had found another.

The heavy rain had stopped and everything seemed to be steaming in the muggy evening air. My hair was soaked and my jeans had wet patches above the knees. My leather jacket was hanging loosely round my shoulders.

Billy was standing with his new friends, leaning against the burger and hot dog stand which had stayed open, pleased, no doubt, with the extra business.

"Hi," I said. "Have you been here all the time?"

Billy nodded his head. "I heard what had happened. I didn't really want to get too close."

I looked him straight in the eye and nodded hurriedly. I understood. It hadn't been long before that when Billy and I had been within metres of a dead boy, his blood running on to the floor like poster paint. I could understand why he hadn't wanted to get close.

"I was a bit surprised that you wanted to go and look."

"I didn't," I said. "I just got swept along."

Perry, Billy's new friend said, "Wanted a look at the blood, did you, Pat?"

I didn't answer. I wasn't keen on the way he assumed first name terms with me. He was an odd kid who I recognized from a youth club some years before. I tried to catch Billy's eye to register dismay at the complete absence of brains in his new found pal, but he was taking a cigarette out and accepting a light from Perry. I looked Perry up and down. His head was almost shaved and he had a light T-shirt on as if it were summer. His tight jeans stopped halfway up his legs, making his DMs look huge and threatening. On his wrist he had a tattoo of the word HATE.

When I had known Perry he had had a baby face

and had been into Dungeons and Dragons. Instead of growing upwards like everyone else he had filled out and now he looked tough enough to chew nails.

He'd been in trouble with the police, I knew that. I'd reminded Billy of it weeks before when he'd started hanging round with him.

"I've been in trouble with the Law as well, Pat," he'd said to me. "Maybe his friends won't want him hanging round with me!"

"But you were innocent!" I'd said, unhappily. I'd noted the fact that Billy had begun to talk about the police as the Law. In the past he'd always defended the police, reminding me of what a hard job they did etc. etc. in difficult circumstances etc. etc. Now he talked about them as though they were an anonymous organization, a faceless group of people who had to be avoided.

I looked around at the police officers nearby scribbling notes on their pads.

"I heard one of the policemen say that it was a single stab wound," I said.

"Straight in, see. Right into the heart," Perry said and did the actions, as though he was a swordsman. I rolled my eyes.

"Who was it?" Billy said.

"A boy called Jack Ross," I said. I'd heard the name bandied about from where I'd been standing.

"Jack Ross!" Perry said, slowly. "Frank Ross is going to be hacked off about that."

"Who's Frank Ross? The kid's brother?"

"Quick detective work, Patsy," Perry said, smirking.

"Pack it in," Billy said, giving Perry a dark look.

"Twin brothers, Frank and Jack Ross. They went to Riverside Boys'," Perry said, "where I used to go."

"You mean you've left school?" I said, sarcastically. It didn't surprise me that Perry had gone to Riverside. It was the roughest school in the area, boys only. There'd been talk of bullying and racist attacks down there.

"His girlfriend was with him when he was stabbed," I said.

"Louise Palmer," Perry said. "They were engaged."

"Engaged! At eighteen?" I said.

"So I heard," Perry said, making mock boxing movements with his fists. "Over here!" he shouted to one of the other boys and began to dance around, ducking his head from time to time as though he was in a fight. He looked like a twelve-year-old. A couple of nearby police officers gave him quizzical looks. Had he no sense of occasion? A boy had died on the pavement, less than a couple of hundred metres away, and Perry was having the time of his life.

"You coming home?" I said, through my teeth, to Billy.

"Yes, sure." Billy took his cigarette out, dropped

it on to the ground and stamped it down.

"See you later," he said in the direction of Perry and the others and walked off with me.

"I don't know how you stick him!" I said. I couldn't help it. I had to say something. It had started to rain again and I put the collar of my jacket up.

"I'm not asking you to be mates with him."

"But why him? Why *him*?" I said, looking up at Billy.

He smiled and put his arm loosely around my shoulder.

"Come on, Patsy. I know you're always looking out for me, but you can't choose my friends. You're not my mum."

"I know but..."

"I like him. He makes me laugh. Anyroad, I met his brother, Darren, when I was on remand. He asked me to look out for him."

"Oh," I said.

"He's not very bright, but he's harmless," he said, his arm still round my shoulder.

We came to the edge of the park and saw the police cars still parked in the street. Around the corner the scene was still busy.

"Did you know the boy, Jack Ross?" I said.

"Nope," Billy said with certainty, taking his arm away, holding back from the police tape that hung from lamppost to lamppost.

"You know he..." I stopped when I saw a small bouquet of flowers on the pavement where Jack Ross had lain. I was going to say that he had had the same leather jacket on as me. I didn't, though. It seemed a stupid, pointless comment to make. I remembered his girlfriend holding tightly on to the arm of one of the paramedics, saying, *He's going to be all right, isn't he? Isn't he?* Even though it was as plain as the nose on her face that he was dead.

"Honestly, Pat," Billy said, "of all people I should think that you've seen enough dead bodies for one lifetime."

He walked off up the street away from the scene of the crime. I saw him talking to a couple of girls standing on the corner. Somebody else new that Billy was acquainted with.

He was right about me, though.

About a year or so previously I'd chosen to go to work in my uncle's detective agency and I'd gotten involved in a number of murder cases. Even though I'd decided to try and make a career out of private investigation work, instead of going to university, I had no great relish for gazing at the scene of a killing.

In spite of myself I felt my eyes swivelling back to the place where it had happened. The police were tidying up and from where I was standing I could see the shape of the body drawn out on the pavement. A chalk outline of the kid's last moments.

It was a strange thing. It was just a place on the street but it would never be the same again. An old iron gate, its paintwork peeling, a sign that said *Wood Road Park*. The local kids would come to it in awe as though it were a special place. They would look intently at the ground where the young man's body had lain, they would concentrate hard recreating the action out of thin air, listening for the distant sounds of the crime. For days and weeks to come, after the police had gone, the old park gate would be haunted by the death and no one would be able to walk past without feeling something about it.

I took a last look at the flowers and walked off up the street towards Billy, pushing my arms into the sleeves of my jacket. I could see the rain in the light of the street lamps, like tiny needles plunging down to the ground.

As I approached Billy, the girls walked off. He was smiling and we began to walk away from the park.

"The police have got the guy who did it!" he said.

"Really?"

"Yep! Turns out it was Lee Cooke. Turns out the girlfriend, Louise Palmer, identified him."

"Oh." That was it then. Cut and dried. "Is he in custody?"

"Yeah. Police picked him up with his brother, Kevin, down by the river."

"Good!" I said, feeling a spurt of satisfaction, a

sense of justice having been done. Someone commits a terrible crime, they are identified by a witness and picked up by the police. It was neat and tidy.

We were coming to the top of my street and I was getting wetter by the second.

"Let's go to the car auctions on Saturday. You might see something you like," I said, walking away from him, down towards my house. "Give me a ring," I shouted, looking back.

He waved at me, a pinprick of light coming from his cigarette, and then he walked off. I lingered, just for a minute, until he was out of sight. Then I went indoors.

# 3

# Back to School

It was Thursday morning, just over a week later, when I got the phone call from my old teacher, Miss Eliot, asking me to go and see her at the school. I'd just walked through the office door that said *ANTHONY HAMER INVESTIGATIONS INC*, when I was faced by my uncle holding a chocolate biscuit in his hand.

"Honestly," I said. "What would Aunt Geraldine say?"

"I had no breakfast this morning! I'm absolutely starving," he said and disappeared through the door into his own office.

My aunt Geraldine had decided that my uncle Tony was putting on far too much weight for a forty-five-year-old man. "Since he left the police force he's not as active as he was!" she'd said to me on the phone. "He's reaching a ripe age for a heart attack!" She'd put him on a calorie-controlled diet so that he would lose weight sensibly, although I frequently found him grabbing unauthorized snacks when no one was looking.

I sat down at my desk and looked proudly, once again, at the new computer in front of me. I clicked the on switch and waited until the screen filled up with colour and icons. My opening message came up: *Good morning, Patsy Kelly. How are you today?* And I smiled stupidly and began to look through the files.

The phone rang and I picked it up, announcing, in my nicest voice, the name of the agency.

"Patsy Kelly, is that you?" the voice said.

"Patsy Kelly speaking," I said, importantly.

"It's Sue Eliot, Miss Eliot from Woods School."

"Oh," I said, surprised.

"I wondered if you could come into school and see me."

"I..."

"I need to talk to you about something important. Some advice..."

I held the receiver away from my ear for a minute. Bossy Miss Eliot wanted some advice from me?

"It's about this Jack Ross business..."

"Oh." The Jack Ross *business*. She meant the murder.

"I can't really talk over the phone. Could you come over at lunchtime today?"

"OK," I said, and was about to say something polite when I heard the click of the receiver being replaced and the long hum of the dialling tone.

My uncle came out of his office. "Patricia, look up some of our old clients on the LAW files. I'm going to do a bit of touting for business."

I moved the mouse and opened up the database. I clicked on *LAW95.doc* and waited while the machine trawled through its files finding the right section. Then in a flash a list of client names and details of their businesses came up on the screen in front of me. It was nothing short of a miracle.

Tony was standing behind me, looking at the screen. He reached across and leant his middle finger lightly on the mouse, manipulating it so that in a few seconds he had opened up several other files. He seemed to be whispering under his breath, talking quietly to himself. I sat back feeling superfluous.

After years of ignoring modern technology my uncle had finally succumbed and bought an office computer. It had been installed a few weeks before and Tony had gone on a couple of courses to learn how to use it. Then he had proceeded to come back and teach me how to use it, as though he were the very expert who had invented it in the first place. He'd gone through it very slowly as though I was a five-year-old child, not a young woman of almost twenty. He'd bought books about computers and several programs that he could use from security companies. Usually pretty careful about money, he'd bought himself a portable lap top that he carried around with him. He had fallen in love with it and was growing into a computer bore.

"I've got to go out about lunchtime," I said.

"Um..." Tony said, still fiddling with the mouse.

"To see my old teacher. She wants to talk to me about the Jack Ross case."

"Jack Ross?" Tony said, only half listening.

"The boy I told you about who got stabbed last week."

"Yes? See Patricia, if you click here and then hold the cursor like this ... you get, just a minute ... you get a completely new document!" His eyes were narrowed and he was looking suspiciously at the screen. When a new document appeared he said, "There!" and stood back looking as though he had just baked a cake.

"It happened at the fireworks display in the park. I was there, do you remember, I told you about it..."

"Make sure it doesn't take too long. We've got a lot of business to drum up." He said it standing at the door of his office, a stern look on his face. "You can't let personal matters spill over into work time."

The door closed gently behind him and for a

minisecond I felt annoyed. Just lately my uncle's mood seemed to change very quickly and I was usually at the receiving end. After a few moments I sat back in my chair and let it ease away, like air from a deflating tyre.

My uncle Tony, Aunt Geraldine, my mum, my dad, they'd all wanted me to go to university, but I'd chosen to stay in my uncle's business and learn to be a private detective. I'd tried hard, learning everything my uncle had to teach me. In my first year in the job, when I'd been just filling in time before university, I'd been drawn into some unpleasant murder cases. I'd felt important, I can't deny it. Ever since I'd decided to take the job seriously, though, there'd been very little business. I'd done some undercover work in a couple of department stores looking for shoplifters; I'd done some phoning around for information on insurance claims, even gone and interviewed some claimants about fires and burglaries; I'd gone door to door asking questions on an armed robbery case for some solicitors my uncle worked for. I'd done a lot of paperwork, ringing up solicitors and big companies to see if they had any business for us.

It was hard to admit it but it hadn't lived up to my expectations.

I looked at my watch. I had three hours to go until my meeting with Miss Eliot. I drew a tiny sigh and went back to the computer.

* * *

Miss Eliot was brusque and straight to the point.

"How much do you know about the stabbing of Jack Ross? What have you read in the paper?"

"Just that it was an argument that got nasty," I said, wondering what the problem was. Jack Ross's girlfriend had identified the attacker as Lee Cooke. He had been charged and was on remand as far as I knew. It had been an open and shut case. The stabbing of a young man by another young man; it was all too frequent.

"Yes, that's true. There are some complications, though. I'd better start at the beginning. Do you want a cup of coffee? I'm parched," she said, and walked off.

I watched as she marched across the staffroom in search of two mugs for coffee. There were about thirty teachers sitting around on chairs and armchairs opening Tupperware boxes, eating sandwiches and drinking from cups or cans. In the far corner of the room several had cigarettes and above them was the distinct fog of tobacco smoke. I was mildly shocked to see some of the faces of the smokers being the pious, strict teachers that had taught me over the years. I also noticed several teachers lounging across chairs, their shoes off and legs splayed comfortably around. The laughter was raucous in places and the conversation peppered with words that would have shocked a vicar.

I remembered when I was much, much younger creeping up to a staffroom door with some message for a teacher, feeling privileged to have been chosen, approaching the staffroom in a hushed way as if it were a kind of church.

Miss Eliot came back with two steaming mugs of dark liquid and started to talk again as though she'd just taken a breath between sentences.

"Louise Palmer, Jack Ross's girlfriend, is a student of mine. She's in year eleven, in my form. It seems that she's been seeing this boy for about a year. The other girls said it was true love, you know the sort of thing." She was rolling her eyes at me, treating me like an equal. I gave a brief, businesslike nod.

"Jack Ross came from Riverside Boys'. You know what a bad reputation that place has. There's not a week goes by without some report of fighting or bullying from there."

"It's a boys-only school," I said, in way of an explanation.

"Yes, and it brings out the worst in them. There's been theft and intimidation and numerous racist incidents in the last few years. Anyway, that's the kind of place Louise Palmer's boyfriend came from. It seems he's a twin. The other boy, Lee Cooke, also had a brother at the school, an older boy, Kevin, I think it was."

"Yes, I'd heard."

"When Louise and her boyfriend were on their way to the fireworks display they came upon Lee Cooke. An argument broke out and Lee stabbed Jack Ross."

"The police picked him up and charged him, didn't they?"

"Yes, he's on remand."

"Right," I said, looking quickly at the clock on the wall behind her. My lunch hour was almost over.

"What happens now apparently is that the police proceed with their enquiries and in a couple of months the case will come to trial and Lee Cooke will be tried for murder. The trouble is..."

I raised my eyebrows while Miss Eliot paused for a moment. Nothing ever goes smoothly, there's always a hitch. She lowered her voice.

"Yesterday Louise Palmer left home. Her mother came to see me this morning, in a terrible state. It seems that all the business with the police and the law courts has frightened Louise and she's told her mother that she's not going to give evidence. The police are furious, Mrs Palmer says."

"Oh," I said.

"Lee Cooke could be released for lack of evidence."

"So the police will have to find her?" I said.

"That's the problem." Miss Eliot sat back in her chair looking tired. "They say they'll put out an alert to other police stations etc. etc. but Louise's mother says that she's afraid of this Kevin Cooke, the older brother. She's afraid that he will find her and do something to her... So if Louise doesn't want to be found..."

"You want me to find her?" I said, the penny finally dropping.

"Yes, sort of. It's not really a case of *looking* for her..."

"Well, certainly, finding missing persons is something done by my uncle's agency. I could contact him and he could see Louise Palmer's mother..." A small glow was forming in my chest. My first actual case. With the lack of work that the agency had, my uncle would be delighted.

"The thing is, Patsy, it's not really a case in that sense. You see, Mrs Palmer can't afford to pay anyone to look for Louise. The woman's recently been made redundant, a one parent family. She hasn't got the money for a tube fare into London, let alone to pay someone to go and find her daughter."

"Oh," I said.

"I suppose what I'm really asking is a favour from you, Patsy."

"I'd have to tell my uncle," I said, remembering my promise to him.

"Louise's mum has a rough idea where she might have gone. It would be good if you went to see her, had a chat. It's not really a *case* as such. It's just that wherever Louise is she's much more likely to come back and testify if a person of her own age persuades her, don't you think?" She nodded her head rapidly as though agreeing with herself.

"I don't know about my uncle..."

"It's a favour, Patsy. I've known this girl and her mother for nearly five years. She's been in trouble from time to time and somehow, with help, I've managed to pull her back on to the right path. I'd hate to lose her now, especially when this is something that's not her fault, where she's the victim."

The sound of a bell made me jump. It went on for almost a minute and everyone in the staffroom seemed to freeze.

"I'll have to ask my uncle. But I'm sure he won't mind me spending a couple of days working on it."

I watched as the teachers stubbed out their cigarettes and rose from their seats. There was a distinct noise of feet and voices from the other side of the staffroom door, as though the school was coming to life again. Picking up her books, Miss Eliot walked me along the corridor to the front of the building.

"This girl needs help and her mother doesn't know what to do," she said, raising her voice above the noise.

"I'll ring you," I shouted, and zigzagged off through the crowds of kids edging their way back into the school.

* * *

"Working for nothing! We're not a charity you know, Patricia!" My uncle was looking hungry, weaving his fingers in and out of each other. He had just come back from a meeting with a solicitors' firm who he'd hoped to get some business from. His grumpy mood suggested that not much had come of it.

"I just thought as we weren't very busy..." I said, quietly.

"We *are* busy. We've got to look for business, Patricia. It's not all chasing murderers, you know. There's another side to this as well," he said and put the end of a biro into his mouth.

"I can still do the clerical work. I just need a few hours. At least to go and see the girl's mother, have a talk to her..."

"We work for people who pay us. That's why it's called a business."

I left him mumbling and chewing at the pen. I walked into my own office and sat down with a thump. I spent what was left of the afternoon writing letters and phoning. At five o'clock exactly I put on my leather jacket, zipped it up and left the office.

When I got home I phoned Miss Eliot at the number she'd given me.

"I'll be able to work the case but only on a casual part-time basis. We're very busy, you see. I'll be doing some work in the evenings if that's OK," I said.

"Great, Patsy. I knew I could depend on you," she said.

I put the phone down and bit my lip, wondering if I'd done the right thing.

# 4

# Louise Palmer

I went to meet Louise Palmer's mother on Friday evening. Brian Martin picked me up in his car and we drove there together through a wet drizzle that had been around all day. I watched as it turned the screen into a fine mist and then was cleared by the tireless arm of the wiper. The people on the streets looked damp, giving up on umbrellas and walking doggedly through shallow puddles that dotted the pavement. The squeegee kid at the traffic lights stood looking depressed as car after car turned down his services.

Mrs Palmer lived on the Riverside Estate, only a few streets from the school that Jack Ross and his brother had gone to. As we drove there, Brian was talking about West Ham. Football was a great passion of his and it was getting on my nerves.

"We're middle of the league right now. The problem is we've got so many injuries that I can't see us pulling ourselves up. What we need is some new players," he said, patting me affectionately on the hand. "It all depends what happens to Sheffield next Saturday..."

I let him talk on for a while, nodding and umming from time to time.

Don't get me wrong, I liked Brian Martin. He'd helped me out on a couple of cases and I'd felt attracted to him, had warmed to him. I'd continued seeing him even after Billy had got out of prison. Lately though he'd begun to get me down and I'd been toying with ways of breaking up with him. A couple of times I'd been on the brink of telling him I didn't want to see him any more but his hurt expression and his affectionate manner made me lose my nerve.

He finished speaking and we drove along in silence for a bit. I put him out of my mind and started thinking about Louise Palmer, wondering where she had gone to. I'd spoken to Billy about it on the phone and he'd told me some things that Perry had told him.

Jack and Frank Ross were identical twin brothers who had left Riverside Boys' just over a year before. Lee Cooke had been in the same year but Kevin, his brother, was a year older. The brothers hadn't hung around together. Some rivalry had grown up over the years between them and they had each got their own group of friends. The Ross boys got on better at school, got better results when they left. Perry said that Frank Ross, the brother of the dead boy, worked in a solicitor's office as a clerk. The Cooke brothers on the other hand spent a lot of their school years down the park, riding their bikes round the streets. They weren't stupid but they went to gyms and played pool instead of studying. Perry had said that they were involved in a lot of bullying and there was a rumour that they'd got into crime. He said that they were thugs and should be avoided. I thought that was rich coming from someone who had HATE tattooed on his wrist but I hadn't said it. I hadn't wanted to upset Billy.

"What do you think, Pat?" Brian's voice interrupted me and I realized that we'd pulled up to the pavement outside the block of flats that we were looking for.

"I'm sorry, I was miles away."

"Is there something wrong? You've hardly listened to a word I've said."

"No. I'm just preoccupied," I said.

"Patsy, are you sure everything is all right? Between us, I mean."

I looked at him and cringed. I knew I should tell him the truth. I opened my mouth to speak just as he leaned across and gave me a quick peck on the lips.

"Let's go and see Mrs Palmer, OK?" I said, forcing a tiny smile.

He walked ahead of me into the flats, a spring in his step. I followed him, my shoulders rounded with guilt. It wasn't the right time to tell him.

Mrs Palmer was older than I'd thought she'd be, in her forties or even fifties. She was small with vivid auburn hair and lipstick to match. She wore a big chunky jumper and leggings and lots of gold jewellery, earrings, rings, necklaces and a charm bracelet. She looked top heavy, her full body balancing on skinny bird-like legs. She moved about lightly as well, as though stepping carefully wherever she went.

"Thank you for coming, dear. Miss Eliot says you're a smart girl. I only hope you can find my Louise."

We sat down on a threadbare settee while Mrs Palmer went off to make a cup of tea. The room was perfectly clean but curiously empty. A TV was in the corner and there were a couple of chairs plus the settee; no hi-fi, no video, no ornaments or pictures. I made a face at Brian to show how dismal it all was and he gave me a half-smile back.

"My Louise, she's very sensitive." I could hear Mrs Palmer coming in. I took a mug of tea and so did Brian. "I don't know what the teacher told you but here's how it is. My Louise, she's a sweet girl but she's had her fair share of trouble. Teachers never liked her, that's the point. Apart from Miss Eliot. The rest of them just made up their minds that she was a bad apple and that was it. Last couple of years she's kept out of trouble. Been a good girl, not like some on this estate."

She lit a cigarette and blew the smoke sideways.

"When she started seeing Jack I was that pleased. He was a lovely boy. He was always buying her stuff. She's got a drawer full of jewellery out there."

She stopped and pulled a tissue out of her sleeve, holding it as though she were about to dab her eyes.

"They'd been going out for nearly a year. He really cared about my Louise. Lovely family as well, dad's in the building trade, that's what Jack was doing, going into his dad's firm. I said to my Louise you stick with him and you'll have a nice detached house in Essex, that's what you'll have."

"When did Louise leave home?" I said, taking my pad out of my bag. It was time to get her talking about the stuff that mattered. She took a while answering. I had it in my mind that she was picturing the detached house in Essex.

"Two days ago."

"Did she leave you a note?"

"No, she phoned me. About eight in the evening. She said she'd seen Kevin Cooke. Said he'd threatened her, told her that if she went to court against their Lee then she wouldn't be looking at her pretty face in the mirror for much longer."

"Did you tell the police?"

"Yes, but they say they can't do anything unless Louise makes a complaint."

"Sue Eliot says that you have a good idea where she might have gone?"

"Yes, probably. I think I know." She stood up and seemed to be making a decision, her arms flapping for an instant at her side. "Come with me into Louise's bedroom. I'll show you her stuff."

The bedroom was a complete contrast to the living room. It was crammed full of furniture, electrical equipment, pictures, ornaments. On the bed were several large cushions and a couple of giant stuffed toys, the kind that cost a fortune.

"My Louise never wanted for nothing, see. When her dad left I looked after her. I was working then. Machinist, good money. They made us redundant though. Two months ago. Things have been hard since then."

"Where do you think she might have gone, Mrs Palmer?" I said, gently, trying to get her to come to the point.

"Here. This is where she keeps all her personal stuff." She pointed to a miniature pine chest of drawers. It was about thirty centimetres high with six small drawers in it. "Up till a few months ago she used to go to dance classes. A place near

Liverpool Street station. She's been going there for two years. She was really good. She made a couple of friends there, you know, from different parts of London. They came round here once or twice but mostly Louise went over to see them. It's not exactly the sort of area you want to bring friends to, is it? I haven't seen either of them for a while but I know she kept in touch. Being as they're out of this area she might have gone to one of them. I didn't think about it at first, didn't mention it to the police, see. I was going to but then I thought, if the police turn up, Louise is liable to run off somewhere else, where I won't be able to find her."

"Right," I said, opening my pad. That made sense. To go somewhere where nobody local could find her. The warbling of the phone sounded from out in the hallway.

"I'd better get that, dear," she said. "You look in those drawers. You'll find the dance school photograph."

As soon as she'd gone I opened the top drawer and saw a number of pairs of earrings and gold chains. I could hear Mrs Palmer's voice from the hallway rising and falling, obviously pleased at whoever had phoned. I pulled open a couple of the other drawers to see if there was any information about the dancing school and found a photograph of a group of dancers in black leotards. There were three of them, two pretty blonde girls and in between them a tall brunette. One of the blondes must have been Louise Palmer. On the back of the photo were the words JINGLES DANCE STUDIO, SPITALFIELDS. Underneath someone had written: *Louise Palmer, Lisa Black, Sherry Stevens, freestyle presentation, May.* It had only been taken six months or so before. Underneath it there was a small, red address book. Flicking through, I saw phone numbers and addresses beside the names of Lisa Black and Sherry Stevens. I jotted them down and held on to the photo.

I couldn't resist having a quick look through the other drawers. They were full of girl's things, creams, lipsticks, combs, hair bands. In the bottom one were some letters.

I hesitated for a minisecond before I took them out of the drawer. I was just being plain nosy really. I had the information I had come for. There was no excuse.

There were three unsigned letters, all on blue paper. I glanced at the headings: *Dear Lou Lou, It's only hours since we were together but already I miss you; Dear Lou Lou, All I think about, all day long, is you; Dear Lou Lou, This is love, don't try to tell me it isn't.* They were carefully composed in neat handwriting. At the bottom of each were the words, *You and me together always* and dozens of kisses.

I was impressed. Nobody had ever written love letters to me. I thought for a brief moment of Brian, sitting on the settee waiting for me to come out, and a feeling of gloom settled on me. I folded the letters up and put them back. It was only fair. I hadn't intended on invading Louise's privacy to that extent. *You and me together always.* It was a passionate way of ending a letter. Jack Ross must have been madly in love. Could I ever love someone that much? To write those kind of words without feeling embarrassed about it? I shook my head and replaced the letters in the drawer just at the moment when Mrs Palmer came back into the room.

"Now, did you find the photo and address book?" she said, breathless.

"Yes, right," I said, with my pad in front of me, trying to sound businesslike. "One thing, Mrs Palmer. If you've got these addresses why don't you go and see Louise yourself?"

"Because of Kevin Cooke, my dear. He knows me. He could follow me, find out where Louise is."

"Is that likely?" I said, imagining a young man following Mrs Palmer. I must have had a funny expression on my face because Mrs Palmer looked momentarily annoyed with me.

"You don't know the Cookes do you, dear?"

"No," I said.

"They're nasty young men, involved in all sorts, stealing, violence, you name it they've done it. They've got a whole gang who hang around with them. They only live two minutes' walk from here, in the tower block. Kevin Cooke or one of his pals will be watching me all the time, seeing where I'm going, you depend on it."

"Right," I said, wondering if she were being paranoid or if the Cooke brothers were Mafiosi apprentices. "Have you got a really recent photograph of Louise?"

"I have," she said and walked away towards another room. I went back into the living room and found Brian looking at the sports pages of the daily paper.

"Here." Mrs Palmer reappeared. She handed me a photo of Louise Palmer and Jack Ross together, smiling at the camera. "You can keep that. I've got a copy."

"This is good," I said, just as a knock on the door sounded. Brian stood up, folding the newspaper up and putting it under a cushion. "We must go, anyway. I'll give you a ring as soon as I find out anything."

"And I'll ring you, you know, if she contacts me."

Mrs Palmer opened the front door and a young man stood there. I looked at him for a moment, not quite believing my eyes. In front of me, in the photo, was Jack Ross, the dead boy. Standing just a few metres away was his double.

"Oh, Frank. Thanks for coming to see me." Mrs Palmer gave the young man a hug.

"This is Patsy Kelly, the girl I told you about.

She's going to try and find Louise. This is Frank Ross, Jack's brother."

"Hello," he said, looking directly at me. He put his hand out.

"Hello. I'm so sorry about your brother," I said, shaking his hand. He was formally dressed in a dark suit with a striped tie, as if he was on his way home from work. He looked older, early twenties at least. I remembered then that he worked in a solicitor's office.

"This is my friend Brian," I said. "I didn't know your brother but I was there at the park on the night he was stabbed. It was terrible."

He nodded his head but looked too upset to speak.

"We must go," I said, aware that we were trespassing on family grief. We edged past the two of them and got out of the flat and into the street.

It was raining again, heavier than before. I zipped up my jacket and couldn't help but look round to see if there was a young man watching Mrs Palmer's house or looking at us in any suspicious way. I had in mind a shady character in dark glasses hiding behind a newspaper. There was no one though, just a couple of kids braving the rain, knocking a football about. Walking towards the car I thought how funny it had been to see Frank Ross in person in front of me, a mirror image of his dead brother. I felt a little shiver and then realized that Brian had put his arm around my shoulder. It was the last thing I felt like, human contact. I quickened my steps towards the car and he followed me.

# 5
# Followed

On Saturday I left home early with my mobile phone in my pocket. I was wearing jeans and my leather jacket. In my rucksack I had a long green plastic mac that I'd recently picked up in a charity shop for fifty pence. I also had a green felt hat with a narrow low brim and black chiffon scarf that was balled up inside it. On top of it all was a letter that I'd written to the missing girl.

I'd had some luck the previous evening. Brian Martin had suggested that I try the phone numbers to see if the girls still lived at those addresses. I rang each of them, pretending I was someone from Jingles Dance Studio. I'd said that I was an ex-pupil and asked them about the whereabouts of another girl, someone I'd lost touch with. Lisa Black's family had moved down to Devon so I crossed her off my list. Sherry Steven's mother said she was out but would be back about ten. I didn't bother to ring back. I just assumed that that was where she would be.

That Saturday morning, I'd got up feeling positive and hopeful. I took the tube then walked to the street that Sherry Stevens lived in. It was a long terrace with three-storey houses on each side. I found her number and walked past and back about half a dozen times, gathering my confidence together. I looked around to see if there was a nearby place that I could stand and wait, where I wouldn't be noticed. There was only a bus stop about fifty metres away. A woman with a baby and a young man in a honey-coloured suede jacket were waiting. It would have to do. I put my hand in my bag and felt the letter there and made my way slowly towards Sherry Stevens' front door.

I'd had some difficulty deciding how to approach the problem. I didn't have the time or resources to follow Sherry until Louise Palmer turned up. I'd opted for a more direct approach. I'd decided to try and flush her out. I took my glasses off and tucked them in my pocket. I knocked on the front door, taking the envelope out of my bag. All the time I was going over my lines in my head. Finally, after what seemed like ages, an older woman answered.

"Yes?" she said politely.

"Is Sherry in?" I said, pleasantly.

"She's upstairs. I'll get her for you," she said. A few minutes later I heard the sound of footsteps coming down the stairs.

"Yes?" Sherry Stevens stood in front of me, a frown on her face as if she had seen through me already. She was tall and thin and had thick black hair pulled together in an off centre ponytail.

"Louise Palmer's mother sent me to see you. I've got a message. She said you would know where she was."

"Louise Palmer?" she said, pronouncing the name slowly. Her face took on a suspicious look. "I haven't seen Louise for months."

"She's written this letter to her," I said, holding out the envelope.

"I've told you, I haven't a clue where she is."

"If you could just pass this on—" I started, but the door slammed in my face. I stood back, shocked. I hadn't expected the rebuff to be quite as sudden.

I bent over and slid the envelope through the letterbox. I heard it drop and walked off up the street. I went as far as I could go without letting the house out of my sight. Ducking in behind a hedgerow, as rapidly as I could, I took my leather jacket off and folded it up. I pulled out the green mac and put it on along with the hat and the black chiffon scarf. I put my glasses on, zipped up my rucksack and walked out again over the road to the bus stop.

I stood there, looking around, glad that the woman with the baby and the young man had gone, hoping that no one else had seen me.

I had the kind of plan that was full of ifs and buts. The letter I had written was brief and just explained who I was and suggested that she rang her mum to confirm it. It also asked her to meet me, somewhere central where we could talk. I'd put my mobile phone number on it. If Louise was actually in Sherry Stevens' house then I expected Sherry to give her the letter. I hoped Louise would read it and then contact me on my mobile phone. If on the other hand Louise was staying at some other address that Sherry had arranged, then I imagined that she would take the letter to her. That's when I would follow her, discreetly, from a distance.

The big but was that she might not be there at all; she might be staying with some other friend that her mum didn't know. That was something that I could do nothing about. I decided to give it about an hour and then go back and knock on Sherry's door again.

I didn't have to wait that long. Sherry Stevens came out of her front door as though she was in a walking race. She had a long tan coat on and it flowed out behind her as she glided off down the street. I waited for a couple of minutes and then started to follow her.

* * *

She walked along past Euston station, stopping at a shop for a can of drink. I tugged my hat down over my forehead and pulled my scarf round my neck. She went briskly on in the direction of King's Cross and I followed, keeping her tan coat and black pony-tail in view some metres ahead.

I felt excited, I have to admit it. I'd followed someone once before who'd led me to a missing girl. It had been my first real experience of detective work and I'd used a disguise of sorts then to avoid being noticed. My plastic mac crinkled as I walked smartly along and my long chiffon scarf had to be wrapped round my neck twice to avoid it flying out.

My hat was feeling hot and I realized that I'd been silly to choose such a heavy one. On top of my wardrobe I had a whole collection of hats that I liked to wear. I'd collected them over the years and some of them sat in old-fashioned hat boxes that my mum had got hold of for me. The rest were sitting stacked on top of each other or perched on their own, looking delicate and ladylike. I usually wore them with jeans or long skirts and DMs. I'd even worn a couple with my zip-up leather jacket, mixing one style with another. My mum call it having No Sense Of Dress. I just liked to look a bit different.

I slowed down as Sherry Stevens stopped at a pelican crossing. There was a newsagent's just by me and I popped in and bought a paper, keeping her in my view all the time. Outside, I stood for a moment looking at the headlines and as the traffic lights changed I allowed her to cross the road and followed her from the opposite side of the street. After a few minutes, walking in the direction of the Angel, I crossed the road and was behind her once again. I took a quick look at my watch. We'd been walking for twenty-five minutes. I wondered where on earth she was taking me.

She took an unexpected left turn and I walked on past for a moment, afraid that she might look back and see me behind her. I counted to ten in my head and doubled back hoping that she was still in sight. She was, just metres up the road. One minute she was walking away from me and then the next she did an about-turn and walked back down the street in my direction. I turned and headed for the nearby window of an antique shop and stood there anxiously, wondering where she was going.

I made myself focus on the items inside the antique shop window, chests of drawers, a lacquered desk, fragile china. I was determined not to look round and let her see me. A miniature rocking horse caught my eye and I found myself looking at its thick tail which reminded me for a moment of the My Little Pony toy I'd had as a child.

That was when I felt the lightest of taps on my shoulder. I turned round and was faced with Sherry Stevens. Several strands of black hair had escaped from her ponytail and were flying around her face.

She had a smile on her lips as she said, "I have to tell you, Patsy Kelly, you need to practise your skills in following someone. I spotted you a mile off."

I was speechless for a moment.

"I ... have to see Louise Palmer," I stuttered. I was dismayed, not quite sure of what was happening, embarrassment creeping up my neck.

"Oh, Louise is gone by now. She'll have packed her bags and slipped away while you were following me through the streets of London. She's miles away."

We were sitting in a small café and Sherry Stevens had dropped her mocking tone. I had just bought two cups of coffee and I placed one in front of her. I was acting nonchalant, as if I didn't care that she had seen through me, as if it had been all part of the plan. I told myself that I was attempting a damage limitation exercise, part of the investigation.

Inside, though, I felt like a complete fool. Louise Palmer had been in that house, only moments away from me. Now she had slipped away to another place that I couldn't know about. And Sherry Stevens would be able to gloat about it.

"Look, Patsy," she said, after a minute, "you have to understand that Louise is terrified of this kid, Kevin Cooke, finding her. He threatened her and frightened her badly. She's going to lie low for a while."

"But her mother only wants to speak to her..."

"Yes, but her mother lives on that estate, close to him. Louise told me that the Cooke boys terrorize people round there and she's sure that if she contacts her mum then he will somehow find out."

"But how could he find out?" I said, nonplussed. She was making Kevin Cooke sound like an intelligence agent.

"Don't look now," she said, "but across the street there's a kid leaning against the wall reading a magazine."

I took a sip of my coffee and let my eyes swivel as far as they could go without turning around. I glimpsed a young man of about eighteen in a suede box jacket. He looked familiar, and then I placed him. It was the young man who I had noticed standing at the bus stop, just before I'd gone up to the house to give Sherry the letter.

"That's Kevin Cooke," Sherry Stevens said.

*That* was Kevin Cooke? He looked ordinary, just like any other kid you might see on his way out shopping or meeting his mates.

"How did he find out where Louise was?" I said, still not understanding.

"He followed *you*, Patsy. Don't you see? You went to see Louise's mum and he followed you!"

"I never saw him," I said, with wonder.

"Of course you never saw him. He's clever, see. It

was Louise who saw him out of the top floor window, just as you came to the door."

"Oh."

"That's why I had to get you and him away while she went off somewhere else."

I felt stupid. Sherry Stevens drained her cup and began to shuffle around in her seat. I knew she was going to get up and leave any moment and I felt that there was something that I should say that could make her see that I wasn't a total incompetent. No words came out of my mouth, though.

"Look on the bright side, Patsy. Louise is somewhere safe now. The very least you can do is pretend you haven't seen Cooke. Let him follow you for a while, let him think that I've told you something and that you're looking for Louise."

I nodded my head.

"You meant well, Patsy, but this whole business is more complicated than you think."

And then she was gone, her tan coat catching in the door as she went out, her ponytail bobbing off down the street.

I left the café about ten minutes later and headed off towards the Angel tube station. I stopped for a minute and bent down to do my DMs up and sneaked a look across the road. He was there still, his back to me, looking in a shop window, just as I had done when Sherry Stevens had come up and tapped me on the shoulder.

I saw the humorous side of it then. I was following her and he was following me. All the while I thought I was being really clever. It was definitely the funniest thing that had happened to me in a while. Excuse me for not laughing.

# 6

# Making Contact

After finally losing Kevin Cooke on the Underground interchange, I decided to go straight round to Billy's. I'd intended to tell him the whole story, but when I got there Perry opened the front door and said that Billy was in the shower. The TV was on in the living room and I plonked myself down in front of it, Perry by my side, exhaling cigarette smoke into a little cloud that seemed to sit in the middle of the room. I looked at my watch and wondered how long Billy was going to be.

After a while Perry said, "That kid whose boyfriend got stabbed last week? Louise Palmer? Her mum's flat got attacked. The window smashed, paint all over the wall."

"No! When?" I said.

"This morning," Perry said, "about eleven, half-past."

"Was she hurt?"

"No, I don't think so. There was a lot of police there, we didn't hang around."

Perry's eyes lit up suddenly as a new programme came on to the screen. He pointed the remote and turned the sound up three or four notches. Loud music boomed out and his face had a look of rapture on it. I left him there and went into the kitchen to wait for Billy.

I went to sit down, but I was agitated by the news he had just given me and ended up pacing the floor. Poor Mrs Palmer. At the back of my mind were the day's events and the fact that I hadn't been able to find Louise. I felt thoroughly dispirited.

The room was dark and dreary and I switched the light on. Even though it was only two o'clock there were grumbling grey clouds in the sky and the air had the smell of damp in it. More rain. It seemed like it had been raining non-stop for weeks. I picked the kettle up from the side and started to fill it. Plugging it in, I opened the fridge to see if there was any milk. There was – just. The only other thing in the fridge was a packet of sausage rolls and a piece of cheese.

Out of nosiness I opened the larder cupboard and saw half a loaf of sliced bread and some tins of beans, spaghetti and frankfurters. At the side of the cupboard were two packs of unopened cigarettes and two Mars bars.

On top of everything else, Billy wasn't looking after himself.

I was reminded of the time over three years before when Billy's parents had been killed in a car crash and he had been left completely on his own. I'd spent a lot of time round his house then, making him do housework, go shopping, keep the ironing up. We'd become best friends. I'd encouraged his interest in cars and helped him buy them at the auctions. I'd watched over the weeks while he transformed them into shiny, near perfect vehicles. He'd helped me a lot too when I'd started working with my uncle, driving me places, offering advice that wasn't always what I wanted to hear.

Our friendship had occasionally sparked into something else. One night, after an important development on a case, I'd been buzzing with excitement and he'd leaned across the front seat of the car, held my face still and kissed me lightly on the lips. It had sent a sudden electric thrill through me, his fingers drawing everlasting circles on my skin.

I'd been thrown, unsure of what to do. When the kiss had ended I'd kept my eyes closed for a minute afraid of saying something embarrassing or stupid. It had happened a couple of times after that; a hug, a kiss, his hand lingering on my arm, his breath on my neck. We'd never done anything about it; we'd turned away, changed the subject and got on with our own lives.

The kettle had boiled so I put a couple of tea bags in some mugs and poured the hot water in.

It was another thing that had changed after he'd been released from prison. Billy's interest in *me* seemed to have dwindled. I had been seeing Brian, of course, so that had put a kind of barrier up between us. Still, though, I'd been disappointed that some of our old closeness hadn't come back.

I watched as the kettle started to boil and let the thought of Brian sit in my head for a moment. I pictured his smiling face and thought about his cheerful voice on the other end of the phone. It simply wasn't enough, just to like someone. I was going to have to find a straight, honest way to finish with him.

I heard the door open behind me.

"Hi," I said, turning round with a mug of tea held out and ready for him. I could smell the dampness and the sweet scent of cologne or aftershave. Without saying anything Billy took the mug of tea.

His hair was still wet. He had jeans on and a shirt that hadn't been done up yet, and his feet were bare. He looked rosy-cheeked and his hair was hanging over his eyes where he hadn't combed it. I felt a powerful urge to push it back with my fingers.

"You're looking a bit hassled," he smiled. "I

thought you were looking for the kid whose boy-friend got stabbed. Did you hear about her mum's house?"

I nodded, glumly. "It's a long story," I said, and picked up my own mug of tea.

After I'd filled him in on my miserable morning, Billy told me some more about the attack on Mrs Palmer.

"Me and Perry were playing snooker at this hall just off the estate. We were going back to my car when there were all these loud shouts and people running. I s'pose it was about eleven, eleven-thirty, something like that. We followed the noise, at least Perry did, so I went along."

Billy playing *snooker*. I just couldn't imagine it.

"The house was in a real mess, the front window smashed and someone had painted the word *grass* over the front door in red paint. The police were there by then, but there was no sign of whoever did it. The word was that three kids pulled up in a car, jumped out, did the damage and then drove away. No one saw them, or if they did they're not saying."

"Did you see Mrs Palmer?"

"The woman who lived there? Yes. She was in a bit of a state, crying and shouting, you know. You can imagine how she was."

He was right. I could.

"When we going, Bill?" The door opened and Perry came in. "All right, Patsy?" he added, obviously having forgotten that he'd greeted me a short time before.

"Where are you going?" I said, disappointed that Billy had other plans. I was sort of hoping that he might come with me to Mrs Palmer's to break the bad news.

"Tottenham. Perry's got some mates over there."

"We might pull some birds!" Perry said.

My mouth fell open. *Pull some birds!* I looked at Billy and he rolled his eyes, knowingly.

"Can you give me a lift over to the Riverside Estate? On your way out?" I said.

"Yes, sure. You could come to Tottenham with us if you want."

"No thanks," I said, giving Perry a dirty look that he failed to notice.

In the car I sat beside Billy. Perry sat in the back. I looked round and saw that he was reading from a superhero comic book.

"Haven't you got a special car seat for him?" I said to Billy, loudly, so that he could hear.

"Pack it in, Patsy," Perry said and lit up a cigarette. The car filled with the smell of sulphur and nicotine. I hugged my rucksack and thought of Mrs Palmer and what I was going to say to her. Then I heard Perry giving a laugh like a hyena at a couple of old age pensioners who were walking along the street.

"You know why men call women 'birds', Perry?" I said, coughing exaggeratedly at the smoke.

"Nah. You tell me, Patsy," he said.

"Because they're always picking up worms."

"Very funny. Ha ha ha, I'm splitting my sides."

Billy dropped me off at the edge of the estate and I was walking through a tiny shopping precinct when I realized that my mobile was ringing. I pulled it out and pushed the connect button.

"Hello?" I said. The phone had been a present from my mum a couple of months before. "To stop you getting into trouble," she'd said when she bought it. "Now you can get in touch with me in an emergency." Since then I'd hardly needed to use it. I carried it round with me, though, liking the way it looked, ringing people up even when I didn't need to.

"Is that Patsy Kelly?" a female voice said.

"Yes."

"It's Lou Palmer. You nearly got me caught this morning!"

Something leapt with delight in my stomach. Louise Palmer ringing me. Maybe all wasn't lost.

"I'm really sorry. I had no idea that I was being followed."

"That was plainly obvious. I could have been injured, attacked. You said in your letter you were a *professional*."

"I am. I just wasn't expecting Kevin Cooke to be so professional. I'll know him better next time." She was right and all I could do was be honest.

"Have you heard about my mum's place?"

"Yes. I'm on my way round to see her now."

"No one believed me when I said how nasty the Cooke twins were. The police, my mum, no one. We'll look after you, they said. I knew that he would get to me. Maybe now they'll understand why I ran off."

"If you came back the both of you would get protection. My guess is they'll move you to a secret address until the trial is over." I'd heard about cases like this from a friend of mine in the police, a woman inspector called Heather Warren. I usually trusted what she said. "You're a major witness. Without you they've got no case."

"They didn't seem that bothered to me."

"That was before your mum's place was attacked. It'd be different now. Look, I've got this friend, a detective inspector. I could take you directly to her. She's really good. She would make sure that you and your mum got looked after."

"I'm not sure. I need to think about it."

"The longer you leave it, the harder it will be. What about your mum? She needs you now. You need each other."

"Your friend. This detective inspector. She's reliable?"

"Absolutely. Louise, you should come in now, as soon as possible," I said, wasting no time.

"OK. I haven't exactly got much of a choice here.

You meet me. On the Central Line platform at Oxford Circus. At eight o'clock tonight. But one thing. You mustn't tell anyone about this yet. Not the police, not my mum, not even your best friend. This is just between you and me. That's the only way I can feel safe."

"I won't. Oxford Circus, eight o'clock."

"How will I know you?" she said.

"I'll be wearing a hat."

"A what?" She sounded incredulous.

"A red felt hat and a black leather jacket."

"Haven't you got any dress sense, Patsy? OK, Oxford Circus. Central Line platform. Eight o'clock and don't tell a soul."

The phone went dead and I found myself looking carefully round the precinct before I made my way off home. All there was was a couple of small girls playing with dolls and toy pushchairs. As long as they weren't working for Kevin Cooke I was all right.

I found myself smiling at my own joke.

# 7

# Underground

I got to Oxford Circus just after seven-thirty. True to my word I was wearing my black leather jacket and red felt hat. In Sainsbury's I might have looked out of place. At Oxford Circus I just merged in with the Saturday night crowd and to tell the truth, amid the garish colours and bizarre make-up, the nose rings and multicoloured hair, my clothes looked conservative.

Getting ready to leave home I'd been faced with a big dilemma.

I knew, from cases I'd been involved with before, that the golden rule was never to work alone. My uncle had hammered the point home often enough. *Tell other people what you're doing, that way if something bad happens someone will know where you are.* In the past, I'd got into difficult, even dangerous, situations because I'd tried to do things on my own.

This time it was different, though. I couldn't exactly tell my uncle where I was going because he had already told me not to work on the case. I never told my mum where I was going anyway because she was always worrying. I usually confided in Billy, but this time I was worried that Perry might find out and that the word would somehow, by some convoluted method, get back to Kevin Cooke, who would turn up at Oxford Circus station just as I was about to meet Louise Palmer.

I'd thought of ringing Heather Warren, this detective inspector I knew from the police. I imagined a situation where the police could actually take me to the station and wait outside, so that as soon as I met Louise she could get into a car and be whisked away to a secret address. I'd been on the brink of dialling Heather's direct number when I'd stopped. The police would have to make arrangements, assign officers. It would be talked about, memos written, diagrams drawn. What if word slipped out? If the Cooke brothers were so powerful, would they not have links to what was going on in the local police? Perhaps word might even leak out by accident. It had happened before, I knew.

I decided to tell Brian Martin. I was ringing him anyway to break our arrangement for the evening.

He wouldn't like it, I knew, but I had no choice. He'd probably say, *Is everything all right between us?* and I'd probably say, *Yes, of course.* It was dishonest, I knew, but it wasn't the right time to finish it. Dialling his number I felt a tightening of the muscles at the back of my neck.

"Brian, it's me," I said.

"Hi. I've just got in. I'm about to jump in the shower and then I'll be on my way round," he said. He sounded breathless as though he really had just walked through the door at that moment.

"Thing is," I said, "I've got to cancel this evening. Something important has come up and I need to fill you in on a few things."

There was a silence as heavy as lead at the other end of the phone.

"Brian, are you there?" I said, after a few seconds.

"I'm here, Patsy." The words were succinctly spoken.

"It's just that this case is developing and I've got to go to Oxford—"

"It's OK, Patsy, you don't have to make excuses. If you don't want to go out just say, *I don't want to go out*. That's fine. I've got things I could be doing this evening..."

"No, Brian—"

"Patsy, you don't have to explain."

"I have to go to Oxford Cir—"

"Very nice for you. I hear they have some good

clubs up there."

"Brian, I have to tell you something..." I raised my voice.

"Just give me a bit more notice before you drop me next time. That way I can make some other arrangements!"

The phone went dead and I looked at the receiver with a heavy heart. I hadn't even been able to tell him where I was going.

I put my hat and my jacket on and popped my head into the living room where my mum was lying on the settee watching a game show on TV. The room was dark with only a single wall light on. I couldn't tell if she was awake or not. I spoke in a loud whisper.

"I'm meeting a friend at Oxford Circus."

She moved slightly and made an "um" sound so I closed the door gently. I picked up the mobile from the hall table and left.

Walking out into the dark street, I had a good look round. There didn't seem to be anyone in sight. A car pulled away from the pavement further along and its lights swung across me before it drove off. A woman was walking towards me with an umbrella up even though it wasn't actually raining. It had been so wet in the past few weeks that people had become surgically attached to their brollies.

I had to be careful. I couldn't afford to be

followed again. I took a long walk to the tube, stopping and looking in several shop windows, making a mental note of people around me: an Asian man walking his dog; two young girls, their arms linked; a young man in a suit and tie. I even doubled back a couple of times and walked away from the tube, stopping to tie my laces or, once, going into a newsagent's to buy something. Coming out of the brilliantly lit shop with a packet of chewing gum, I was faced with an empty black street and the wet spray of drizzle on my glasses. The street lamps hung like yellow lollipops and the sound of cars splashing in my ears gave me an odd, seaside feeling. One last look into the dark persuaded me that no one was there. Unless the invisible man was following me, I was OK.

I took the Central Line straight to Oxford Circus and arrived half an hour early. I hung around on the platform counting the minutes. I felt good, pleased with myself. I'd persuaded Louise to do the sensible thing. A couple of minutes later my mood changed and I began to worry. She had said she would meet me on the Central Line platform but she hadn't said whether it would be the eastward one or the westward. Where should I wait? What if I was waiting on one platform and she was on the other? A few minutes later I found a linking tunnel and I felt calm again. Then a train came in and thousands of people seemed to get off it. Would I be able to see her, among the crowds? Maybe I should have asked her what she was wearing?

I made myself count from one to ten and back again. All I needed to do was breathe deeply. What could be so hard about that?

It was still only seven-forty-five.

I wondered where Louise Palmer was at that very minute. Was she already on a train looking discreetly at other passengers? Afraid that Kevin Cooke would come and find her?

The Cooke brothers. Everyone had made them sound like the Krays.

How could two teenage boys terrorize an estate? Frighten people into doing things they didn't want to do? I thought back to my old school days and remembered a couple of older boys who'd made careers out of pushing everyone else around, slapping the young kids into shape, making them get up and give them their seats in the dining hall. One of these boys was a nasty kid called Denny Bishop. He had an older brother who hung round the perimeter fence of the building, straddling his motor bike, looking meanly at people through the chicken wire. Denny was always threatening to turn his brother loose on anyone who didn't do what he said. Once or twice, Billy said that we should report him to the Head but none of us really had the guts. So we'd avoided him, ignored his teasing of younger kids, turning away when he became unpleasant.

One day we heard that his brother had been beaten up by some older men and was in hospital in bad shape. The word was that someone else's big brother had got him and we'd all had a private laugh about it. His brother had never come out of hospital, though, and there'd been rumours of wheelchairs and brain damage. Denny Bishop had seemed to visibly shrink in size and began to stay away from school. No one ever heard anything more about his brother.

I heard the distant rumbling of a train, like thunder that was a long way off. A rush of air hit my face and several people who'd been standing around began to move towards the incoming train. One man, reading a newspaper, seemed to stand only centimetres from the very edge of the platform. It made me feel funny to see him there, so preoccupied with his newspaper, unconcerned that he was a breath away from the dark track and the oncoming train. I looked away at someone else and felt a wind hit my face and pull my hair back.

There was a moment's anticipation and then the train hurtled out of the black tunnel, its brakes screeching to such a high pitch that I felt my eardrums ringing.

The doors opened and a multitude of people poured on to the platform, some looking bleary-eyed and uncomfortable, as though they'd just been folded up in a box; others positively bursting out of the doors, looking forward, no doubt, to their evening ahead. I scanned them looking for a blonde girl. I couldn't see anyone familiar, so I got the photos I had out of my bag and looked at them again as the doors seemed to close wearily and with an effort the train moved out of the station.

I walked through to the parallel platform and watched two other trains come in and go out again. As the crowds moved away I noticed a young family struggling to get past. There was a woman wheeling a pushchair that had two toddlers in it. A man was walking distractedly behind her. Tied to the handle-bars of the pushchair were two red balloons that had the Planet Hollywood logo across them. The family looked weary but content and the mother was talking softly to the tiny children, while the father straightened the string on one of the balloons. I couldn't help but watch them. A train rushed out of the tunnel then, surprising me, forcing my hair across my glasses and almost taking my hat off my head.

The young family didn't get on it, but stood leaning against the wall while a straggle of people got out of the carriages.

I thought I saw Louise Palmer then.

I lifted my hand to wave, but stopped myself. I couldn't be a hundred per cent sure that it was her. The train left and I moved forward, passing the woman with the pushchair, her husband kneeling down, still fiddling with the string of one of the balloons. I decided to go along the platform and stand still. I'd told Louise Palmer what I'd be wearing. She would notice me, I was sure.

The blonde girl stood in one place and I watched her through the gathering groups of passengers who had trickled on to the platform. She looked at her watch and half turned in my direction. Her gaze settled on me and I saw her face break into a tiny smile as she started to walk towards me.

From far away, deep into the tunnel, I could hear another train coming towards us. I could *feel* it rumbling deep down, making my nerve ends vibrate. I had to move from side to side to keep my eye on Louise as people got in my way, zigzagging up the platform to get to where they wanted to go.

She waved and I could see her much more clearly, walking tall and proudly towards me, a couple of men giving her long looks as she passed by them.

A group of people spilled down the stairs and frolicked out on to the platform; teenage girls and boys, a whole party of about thirty of them speaking a foreign language, German or Dutch, I wasn't sure. They crowded in front of me blocking my view of Louise. Their leader came down and they crammed around him making a barrier across the platform, which I began to push through crossly, still holding Louise's face in my view, getting closer every moment.

A cold breeze began to chill my skin and I heard, in the distance, the blast of the train building up. I was being moved by the crowds that were edging around the party of students and their leader.

An unexpected thing happened.

A red balloon floated past my shoulder and up towards the roof of the platform. It caught my eye and I watched it, along with everyone else. Many of the young students were pointing up at it and laughing. I looked behind and saw that the family with the toddlers were looking nonplussed as the balloon floated upwards out of their reach and stopped at the highest point of the ceiling. Even Louise Palmer was looking as it hung in the air, the string looking like the tail of some peculiar fish. She looked back at me and smiled for a moment before her expression changed. Her eyes creased up and her mouth hung open in a gesture of surprise.

I didn't understand at first.

She turned her back and began to walk off, pushing her way through the dozens of people who had their necks arched, looking at the red balloon.

And then I knew. She had seen someone behind me.

I turned round, looking for a familiar face, but there were too many people to see clearly. The thundering of the train was in the back of my head, louder than before, like some giant rocket that was going to explode out of the tunnel. The red balloon was being blown frantically here and there. Everyone's face began to look familiar and I looked hard to see if one of them was Kevin Cooke. I turned back and could see Louise Palmer's blonde head bobbing up and down. Was someone following her? I couldn't tell. A big, wide man moved in front of me and she disappeared from my sight. The train stampeded into the station, its noise drowning everything, its brakes sending out a high-pitched wail that seemed like a cry of pain. Then there was a deep silence.

The screaming started a couple of seconds later.

It came from further down the platform. It started with two or three voices and seemed to spread from one to another until there were several people crying. The carriage doors hadn't opened yet and everyone was standing in a kind of frozen picture. Inside the train, people were knocking on the windows, impatient to get out.

I thought a fight had broken out and felt myself being pushed about, moved here and there. It was the last thing I needed, some kind of physical brawl that would stop me finding Louise Palmer. She had been so close. *So close!*

It only took a couple of seconds for the word to reach me.

*"Someone's gone under the train!"*

"What?" I said, stupidly, my eye caught again by the red balloon floating blithely by.

*"SOME GIRL'S THROWN HERSELF UNDER THE TRAIN!"*

My ribcage began to feel heavy, my stomach weighed down with foreboding. A terrible sound came along the platform. The crowds opened to let the train driver through. He was half walking, half stumbling, crying out, a choking sound coming from his mouth. People rushed to him, held him up by the arm. All around the question kept echoing in my ear: *"What's happened?"*

A girl had gone underneath the train. That was bad enough. It couldn't be Louise Palmer, though, I said to myself. It couldn't be her, it couldn't be.

# 8

# Argument

Some of us were taken off the platform and put on the escalator. It reminded me of a school trip. A long snake of stunned people moving upwards away from the stationary train and the dark tracks below. Several London Underground workers were organizing, directing, comforting distressed passengers. Around me there were whispered testimonies.

*"That lady in the green over there, she was just beside the girl. She came running at her, she said, looking distraught. They do, these suicides, you know. Pretty girl, long blonde hair, tall like a model. The man in the suit said she tripped, lost her footing, but I don't know..."*

*"She almost took a couple of people with her. That's what it looked like."*

*"She won't have felt anything. That's a mercy."*

I stood quite still on the escalator, taking breaths in spoonfuls. The woman behind was leaning across me to talk to the woman in front. All the while I was looking down at the scurrying officials at the bottom of the escalators. Several policemen and women had arrived by then.

*"The platform was crowded, though. You can't tell me that's safe, hundreds of people crowding into that small space. It surprises me that there aren't more accidents."*

We were travelling further away from the tunnels and the trains. I could feel the night air from the street mixing with the heat from the station. Across the way I could see two paramedics carrying their equipment on the down escalator.

*"Could she still be alive?"*

*"You can't tell me she's alive. Once you're hit by a train that's you finished."*

"They're for the passengers," I said, hearing my own voice for the first time since it happened. "Some of them are hysterical."

*"It's no wonder. You can't tell me you could watch a young girl fall under the wheels of a train and not feel ill."*

*"I won't sleep tonight. That woman in the green, she definitely won't sleep tonight."*

Then we were at the top of the escalator, thrown rudely off into the ticket area. Several of the passengers around me stood in a small group continuing to talk. A number of other people, guessing that something had happened were pointing across, whispering to each other. A weary London Underground worker was writing on a white board with a black felt.

LONDON UNDERGROUND APOLOGIZES FOR THE DELAY ON THE CENTRAL LINE EASTBOUND. PLEASE FIND ALTERNATIVE ROUTES IF POSSIBLE.

I stood for a while looking at the neat black writing on the white board, my thoughts frozen in my head. One minute Louise Palmer was there, heading towards me, going to the police and finding safety. The next minute she was gone. I had an image of her blonde hair and long coat billowing out behind her as she fell in front of the train. I closed my eyes and ground my teeth together in an effort not to picture what had happened to her. In my mind she had just disintegrated, like fairy dust.

More people were standing round looking at the sign. Several of them were moaning loudly. "*Honestly, more delays! You pay for your ticket and what do you get? Delays and more delays. This is typical of London Underground! I'll be late. I'm writing to complain. It's the third time this week...*"

How long would it take them to clear the track? Whose job was it? I shook my head and headed towards one of the exits, but then changed my mind and walked in the direction of another. I stopped after a few steps and stood aimlessly in the middle of the passers-by. Where was I going? My legs began to feel weak and a growing sense of shock was weighing me down.

Louise Palmer was dead. The word seemed like a tonne weight that had dropped from a great height. She had tumbled under the train, like a tin can or a piece of wrapping paper that someone had carelessly thrown away. All at once she was heading towards me, and then in the space of a second she had turned and was running away. I closed my eyes and remembered it: she looked up at the red balloon and her eyes flicked back at me as she smiled for a second. Then she saw someone she knew, behind me, over my shoulder. She turned immediately and started to move away. I lost her then. In the confusion and the crowds, amid the deafening noise of the train, she seemed to disappear into thin air. Dead, like a heavy metal door slamming shut.

Several people passed by while I was standing like that, one or two bumping into me. I backed up against a wall and looked around. New people were coming into the station every minute, their umbrellas flapping, their faces flushed, off out for the evening, linking arms with their friends and giggling.

Had Louise lost her balance and toppled over? Or had a hand reached out and shoved her off? I put the palm of my hand over my mouth. Train drivers never forget the people who throw themselves in front of them, that's what I've heard. Every time they pass the place again they're faced with the memory of the person whose face they saw only for a microsecond; like a ghostly replay, they see it week in, week out. The thought of it gave me a cold feeling and I spent some minutes trying to zip up my leather jacket and failing to do it. What was I going to do? I needed to speak to someone, tell them what I knew, explain to them why she was there and why I was there.

I walked towards the other wall and leant against it for a minute, feeling near to tears. After a few moments, I stood up straight and tried to pull myself together. A noise distracted me, like an argument, coming from the other end of the ticket office.

I saw two young men facing each other. One of them was black, the other white. I walked towards the area where they were standing and found myself among a small gathering crowd. I stood watching, my mind drifting blankly along. The black kid was taller than the other. His head was almost completely shaved and he had the letter H sculpted on to the area above his ear. He was wearing sports clothes, a grey hooded sweatshirt and joggers.

The white kid looked smarter, was wearing a jacket and trousers and smiling around at the crowd for support. All at once, I recognized him. It was Kevin Cooke. Like a flash of lightning, I suddenly knew him. Lee Cooke's older brother, who had followed me that morning, who had threatened Louise. An invisible hand seemed to thrust me backwards until I was standing near a post, looking on from a distance.

Had he followed me again? Had Kevin Cooke been there, in the dark, shadowing me through the streets? It wasn't possible. It couldn't have been so. I'd been sure that nobody was behind me.

The noise was getting louder, the black kid's voice raised angrily. There were swearwords and pointed fingers and I could see a couple of grumpy-looking policemen coming along and walking to the middle of the fracas. Each of them stood in front of one of the kids and I could see their mouths opening and shutting. Kevin Cooke was standing listening, opening his mouth from time to time as if to interrupt, but stopping as the policeman spoke across him. Unlike that morning, I had a chance to look closely at his face for a few seconds. In the back of my head I could hear the black kid's voice rising.

Kevin Cooke was baby-faced, his cheeks puffed out, no sideburns or beard, his skin pale. Unlike the black kid I couldn't hear his voice. His lips moved, but I guessed that he was speaking very softly. From time to time his eyes seemed to flick in my direction and I moved back, behind the post.

The black kid was walking away, the PC's hand gently on his arm. He was nodding his head and looked as though he had calmed down. Kevin Cooke was still remonstrating, saying something to the policeman with his arm out in mid-air.

Had he followed me on to the platform? I thought about it for a moment. I had been so intent looking for Louise to get off a train that perhaps I hadn't noticed him there, among the crowds. When Louise Palmer had looked over my shoulder she had seen him. That's why she turned and ran away.

I had led him to her.

It was too much to take in. I turned and half ran, half walked out of the station, taking the steps two at a time. Outside, the rain hit me like a cold shower. I stood in it for a minute, letting it wet my face and splatter my glasses. I put my hand up to my head and felt the red hat that was still there. I pulled it off and folded it up inside my jacket. A bus splashed past, signposted for Walthamstow. I jumped on it, chewing at my nails and wondering where I was going to go.

# 9

# Black and White

I waited outside Billy's house for nearly two hours. I used the mobile to ring my mum and tell her I wouldn't be back home that evening, that I was staying with a friend. I sat on the wall and let the rain soak through me.

Once, some years before, I had had a key to Billy's house. He'd given it to me in case I'd gone round to see him and he'd been out testing a car or getting some shopping. I'd used it lots of times without thinking, gone into his kitchen and put the kettle on, clicked the radio on, used the phone to tell my mum where I was.

Somewhere along the line I'd become awkward about it. Probably around the time when we'd had our first kiss. Then there'd been a second and a third. A certain shyness had grown. Instead of just bouncing in, I'd felt embarrassed to walk into his home when he wasn't there. It seemed presumptuous, as though I was assuming that I had rights over him. When he'd been in prison, I'd gone round to check on things. Since then, not at all. I wasn't even sure where the key was any more.

I didn't have to sit in the rain. I knew that. I could have stood in the porch and waited. The rain felt good, though, pricking at my skin, washing through me, bouncing off my jacket, soaking into my jeans. When the traffic was quiet, I could hear the soft pitter patter of it on the windows.

Had Kevin Cooke pushed Louise Palmer under the tube train? The question kept repeating itself in my head. From time to time I got off the wall and walked up and down with annoyance. I had taken precautions against being followed. I had been sure, so sure, that nobody was behind me. How could I have not noticed him?

But then I hadn't seen him that morning when I had thought I was following Sherry Stevens. I pictured him standing in the ticket area, facing the young black man who was arguing so angrily with him.

He must have followed me to Oxford Circus station. I made myself think hard, to the moment when Louise Palmer's expression had changed. I'd looked round on the platform behind me, only for a split second. Had he been there? Among the crowd of kids who had filled up the platform?

I honestly couldn't say for sure that I had seen him there.

I sat down on the wet wall when a woman came out of her house across the way and started to sweep her path. Eleven o'clock on a Saturday night was a funny time to be house-proud. She was probably just keeping an eye on me.

I wondered what was happening at the station. Had they identified her? Would her mother know yet? I imagined Mrs Palmer sitting in all her jewellery in that bare living room, the silhouette of a policeman against the outside window. Maybe she had a WPC with her, because of the attack. I thought of her round body and her spindly legs, like an odd-shaped bird fussing about, and I felt this sadness welling up inside me.

Along the street I vaguely picked out a pair of headlights coming closer, their edges blurred, the rain visible in the beams of light. Poor Mrs Palmer. She had asked me to help her and I hadn't been able to. I'd have to face her, and the police. The car pulled to a halt and I waited while Billy got out. He took a moment to see me, and then I saw, with dismay, that Perry was with him.

"Patsy!" he said, coming towards me. "You're completely soaked."

His face registered concern and I knew I must have looked pathetic.

"What's the matter?" he said.

"Something awful has happened," I said. I opened my mouth to get the next words out but nothing came, so I just walked towards Billy with my arms out and hugged him tightly, my wet hair on his jacket.

"Come on, Patsy, let's go inside," he whispered.

I had a mug of hot, sweet tea in my hand. Around my hair, turban-style was a towel. My jeans were hanging over the radiator and I had a pair of Billy's jogging bottoms on, the ends rolled up. My top half was dry and my leather jacket was hanging around the back of a chair, still glistening with wet droplets. On the table, sat my red felt hat and my glasses, looking like a still life that someone was about to paint.

Perry looked genuinely dumbstruck. Amazingly, he'd said nothing while I'd been telling Billy the story. When I stopped, he spoke quietly.

"Lou Palmer. Dead. That's a turn up. You're sure it was her?"

"I saw her running away."

"It could have been anyone on the platform."

"I'm positive it was her." I raised my voice more than I meant to.

"OK," Billy said. "Let's say it was her. You said some people thought she fell or threw herself off. Couldn't that be the explanation?"

"But if Kevin Cooke was there? That's a hell of a coincidence, isn't it?"

"You don't know for sure that he was there, on the platform."

"No," I said. He was right. I'd seen Cooke in the ticket office, but I hadn't seen him on the platform.

"Just supposing it was Kevin Cooke on the platform. What does that prove? That Louise Palmer fell off the platform because she was running away from him?"

Billy was in a debating mood. He carried on and I listened, all the time my mind bubbling with possibilities.

"He may not have gone near the platform. He may have lost you in the crowds and gone up to the ticket office, figuring that if you or Louise were coming in or out of the station he would see you there."

"He could have lost me." I repeated his words. "He could have, you're right."

It was a comforting thought. Perhaps he hadn't been anywhere near the platform when Louise died. Maybe I hadn't led him to her after all.

"Nope," Perry said, after a few moments, "not Kevin Cooke. He wouldn't have stood around waiting for the two of you to turn up. Not after going to all the trouble of following you. You and Louise could have got on any one of a half a dozen trains and been miles away from there within minutes. Nope, if Kevin Cooke went there to see Louise he'd have looked for you both."

"So he could have come on to the platform," I said, dully. We had come full circle. Back to where we'd started.

"More than likely," Perry said, no hint of a smile on his face.

"Let's say he was on the platform and did have something to do with Louise's death," Billy said. "Wouldn't he have got away, as quickly as possible?"

"Yes," I said.

"Then why would he be hanging around in the ticket office, only minutes after she had died?"

"He wasn't exactly hanging round, he'd got into an argument with this black kid."

"Black kid?" Perry repeated.

"Some young bloke. It looked nasty."

"What did he look like?" Perry said.

"Tall, thin." I tried to picture him. "He had the letter 'H' shaved into his hair. It was very public, everyone was looking."

"Joey Hooper," Perry said. "It must have been Joey Hooper. Him and his brother Paul used to go to Riverside Boys'. They didn't exactly get on with Lee and Kev. Like a *race* thing."

"The Cookes were racists?" Billy said.

"Yep. Lee and Kevin, they didn't like the black kids. Their dad was the same. He was always going on about how there was too many blacks in Britain."

"What's this got to do with anything?" I said, frustration in my voice. I could see the subject disintegrating in front of my eyes. "What about this boy, Joey Hooper?"

"It's a longish story," Perry said, shrugging his shoulders.

"For goodness' sake, Perry, tell us. It's not like we've got much else going on," I said, giving Perry what I hoped was a withering look.

Billy took a packet of cigarettes out and threw them across to Perry.

"Joey and his older brother Paul Hooper didn't get on with the Cookes. They moved out of the area about two years ago. Over to Highbury. They was always Arsenal supporters anyroad," he said, smiling at Billy.

Perry's face was softer, the smile giving him a more grown-up look. He even sounded different, all the usual sarcasm gone from his voice.

"I got on all right with the Hoopers, lots of people did, but their mum and dad couldn't take the racial abuse that they got on the estate, and so they moved to Highbury. They went to a different school and we didn't see much of them. My brother Darren hung around with Paul, Joey's older brother, for a while, before he got sent down."

I listened to Perry's words carefully. I was looking for some connection to Louise Palmer. For the life of me I couldn't see any.

"Trouble was Lee and Kevin Cooke hated them. They used to go over to Highbury, to the places that Paul and Joey went to, just to stir up trouble. It was like a bit of fun for them. About six months ago Joey's brother Paul got badly beaten up down an alley. No one saw what happened or who did it. He was outnumbered, two maybe three kids, and he's never opened his eyes since. The word is that it was Lee and Kevin Cooke."

It was true then what people had said about the Cookes. They really were a dangerous pair.

"Paul never recovered. He's been in a coma for six months. They don't know if he ever will wake up. Joey Hooper swore it was the Cooke brothers who did it, but he's got no proof."

"But what's that got to do with this case?" I said. I couldn't keep the slight edge out of my voice and Perry gave me a hurt look.

"Joey Hooper follows them. The Cookes, I mean."

"What do you mean *follows them*? Everywhere? How can he?" I said.

"No, not everywhere. Just now and then. When they're not expecting it. He just shadows them, then turns up, lets them know he's been there."

"Like a stalker?" Billy said.

"Yes, that's it, like a stalker."

"So what are you saying?" I said, refusing to see what was plainly in front of me.

Perry gave Billy a look of great patience. Then he

took a deep breath and leant forward, his cigarette pointing at me.

"You want to know whether Kevin Cooke was on the platform or not. If Joey Hooper was there, then he must have been following him. If anyone will know what Cooke's movements were it'll be Joey Hooper."

I sat silently for a moment and let it all percolate through. He was right. The black kid, Joey Hooper, he would know, once and for all, whether Kevin Cooke had gone anywhere near Louise. I looked at Perry and felt this great rush of gratitude.

"Can I meet this Joey Hooper?" I said, using the nicest voice I could manage.

"I'm going to see him tomorrow up the London Hospital. To visit Paul."

"Can I come?" I said, tentatively.

"Patsy, you just can't turn up at the hospital. This boy is in a coma, his brother's probably grief-stricken. It's insensitive, it's not right," Billy said, an affronted look on his face.

"No, Bill. She can come. Thing is, Joey will be happy to talk about the Cookes. Most of the time he talks about nothing else. He's obsessed with them."

*Obsessed.* It was a big word for Perry.

"Thanks," I said.

All I needed was for Joey Hooper to place Kevin Cooke on the platform just before Louise fell under the train. It wasn't much to ask.

# 10
## Joey Hooper

It was on the local news the next morning. My mum had the radio on in the kitchen when I got back from Billy's. She was sitting with Gerry, her boyfriend, poring over the Sunday papers. Gerry, a mature student at her college, was reading the book reviews section and my mum was looking at the sports pages.

"Have a nice time last night, love?" she said. She had a triangle of toast in her hand and was painting it neatly with butter.

"Um," I said non-committally. She'd know soon enough.

"Out on the town, were you, Pats?" Gerry said. He had added an "s" on to my name the moment he met me. Six months later it was still annoying.

"Ssh," I said, catching a familiar name from the radio. I turned up the volume.

"*...dead boy's girlfriend, Louise Palmer, fell on to the tracks of the Central Line last night at Oxford Circus...*"

"That's where you were!" my mum said, pointing the toast, like an arrow, in my direction.

"Ssh!" I said.

"*Eighteen-year-old Jack Ross was stabbed two weeks ago outside a local park. An arrest was subsequently made. Due to the death of Louise Palmer, it is now feared that the prosecution case will collapse. Police sources are not able to specify whether the death was due to accident or suicide. Later in the programme we look into the issue of London Transport safety. Why are there no checks on the number of passengers allowed on the platforms at any one time...*"

"Patsy, isn't that the girl whose mother you went to see?" my mum said, her forehead crinkling up.

"Yes, it was," I said. "I'm going to see the police this afternoon."

"Were you there? On the platform?"

"No, no," I lied.

"I knew someone who fell in front of a train once, Pats," Gerry said, leaning back in his chair. "Sad, lonely guy. Nothing to live for." He was shaking his head. "It's a quick way to go, I'll say that."

"Yeah, right," I said. "I'm off for a shower."

"Patsy..." My mum's voice followed me out of the door and part of the way up the stairs.

* * *

I stood in the shower for about ten minutes. The water was scalding, the steam rising up like a fog. I made myself stay there until the heat took away the tension in my back and the stiffness in my neck from where I'd slept on Billy's sofa.

Afterwards, I sat on the bed in my dressing gown, a towel wrapped around my head, my arms folded across my chest. I pushed my feet under the duvet and stayed in that position for some minutes.

I was sure that Louise Palmer hadn't committed suicide. Her boyfriend had been murdered and she had run away after being threatened, those things were true. But from the impression her friend Sherry had given me and the sound of Louise's own voice on the phone, I was sure she wasn't *depressed* or *suicidal*. She'd sounded gutsy, angry even. When I'd seen her, further along the platform, she'd smiled confidently, as if things were going right. I didn't know Louise Palmer personally, but from my very short acquaintance with her she'd seemed determined, mindful of her own safety. That didn't sound like someone who would commit suicide.

Was she pushed?

She had certainly seen someone she knew behind me. She had turned and moved away very quickly. I hadn't actually seen her, but in my mind I imagined her running, skirting round or pushing past people, perhaps in her panic running towards the edge of the platform instead of the exit. Had someone caught up with Louise? Pushed her?

Or was it just an accident?

I had to know whether Kevin Cooke was there or not. The truth seemed to hinge on that. That's why it was important to talk to Joey Hooper, the black kid, whose brother was lying in a hospital bed.

I looked at my bedside clock. It was 11:50 and I was due to meet Perry at Whitechapel tube station at one o'clock. Billy was picking us up later at three. We had a couple of hours in which to talk to Joey Hooper. Perry was sure that would be enough.

For once it wasn't raining, although the charcoal colour of the sky suggested that there was more in store. People were wearing their macs anyway. I wore my leather jacket and a long skirt. Perry walked along in only shirt sleeves. There was a bounce in his step, as if he had springs underneath his boots.

"Aren't you cold?" I said, like someone's mum.

"Nope. Warm-blooded, me," he said cockily, as though I'd just noticed something really special about him. I felt the usual irritation rising up, but pushed it away and followed him across the road towards a massive old building that looked like a church. A noise from above made us look up to see a helicopter rise off the roof, hang in the sky for a few nervous moments, and then shoot off in the direction of the city.

"This hospital was built in 1757," Perry said. "We done a project on it at school."

"Yeah?" I whispered, walking up the majestic steps to the door. It was impressive, like the entrance of some important art gallery or museum.

"Do you know that the bones of the Elephant Man are kept here?" Perry was pointing down, as though he knew exactly where they were kept.

"Really?" I said, impressed.

"Michael Jackson wanted to buy them," Perry went on. "Was willing to pay millions."

There was no answer to that. Perry was looking thoughtfully round the reception area, ignoring the nurses and paramedics who were briskly walking by. He looked as though he were about to launch into eighteen other things that I didn't know about the London Hospital.

"Anyway," I said, wanting to get on. "What about Joey Hooper? Where will he be?"

"Up the top, Nelson Ward," Perry said, his eyes still locked on the floor, his thoughts probably with Michael Jackson and the Elephant Man.

"Come on," I said, taking his arm gently. His skin was soft and I felt like a mum pulling a child along. Waiting for the lift, I said, "Were your brother and Paul Hooper good friends?"

"They used to hang round at Riverside. When the Hoopers moved he kept in touch. After Paul Hooper got beaten up, he brought me here to see him. Then he got sent down, so I said I'd keep in touch. I come here every couple of weeks."

We walked out of the lift and down a long corridor to a sign that said *Nelson Ward*. It was a long room, like a dormitory, the ceiling high enough to house another floor of beds. Perry walked confidently forward. I crept after him, looking from bed to bed, expecting to see a very sick black teenager, his brother sitting by him. It was mostly full of older men, though, some tucked up in bed, looking vacant, smoothing their own covers down; others were sitting in the armchairs beside their beds, reading a newspaper, their arms joined by plastic to a drip on a stand.

We got to a small side ward and Perry stopped.

"You wait here. I have to check with Joey."

The wall that partitioned it off from the rest was half glass and half wood and I could see through to the bed inside. A very thin boy lay there, on his back, his eyes closed. Beside him stood the kid that I had seen at Oxford Circus ticket office, arguing with Kevin Cooke. He smiled when he saw Perry, bending down slightly to put his arm loosely round Perry's shoulder. I watched as he listened while Perry pointed me out through the window. Joey Hooper's head raised slowly and his eyes rested on me, heavy and serious. I had to look away but I still felt the intensity of his stare.

The boy in the bed looked younger than him,

smaller, almost like a schoolkid. There were no machines attached to him that I could see. He was just lying as still as a statue. Perry eventually came out of the small room and talked to me in a whisper.

"Joey'll speak to you. He's just spending some time with Paul and he'll be out."

We stood and watched while Joey Hooper talked to his brother. He sat on the side of the bed and held the sleeping boy's hand. I could see his lips moving as the one-sided conversation went on.

"If you talk to them, people in a coma I mean, they might wake up," Perry said in a whispered voice.

"How old is Paul?" I said, looking at the slightly built boy in the bed.

"Nineteen."

"He doesn't look it."

"Nope. He used to be much bigger. He's lost weight. My brother Darren said that Paul was an excellent bloke. Brilliant muscles, did weights."

Without any warning, Joey Hooper got up, rubbed the back of his hand against his brother's forehead, and walked out of the room. He took a minute closing the door quietly, as though his brother was really just asleep and he didn't want to wake him.

"This is Patsy, is it?" he said with a forced smile. "You want to know some stuff about Kevin Cooke? I got plenty to tell you about him. Where shall we start?"

* * *

We were in the hospital cafeteria. I had a can of Coke, Perry had a sandwich in a plastic triangle and Joey Hooper was staring into a cup of tea. I was sitting at his side and could look at the H that had been painstakingly etched in his hair by some artistic barber. He was sitting straight, looking calm and thoughtful, quite different from the cheeky young man who'd been arguing furiously the previous evening. I started to speak a couple of times but stopped. I thought that he was probably thinking about his brother.

Around us were the relatives of the sick, people with bunches of flowers and worried expressions. I noticed a woman in the far corner, crying quietly to herself. I felt distinctly uncomfortable. After a few moments I decided to speak.

"I saw you last night, down at Oxford Circus, just after Louise Palmer was killed."

"Yeah. I was there," he said, looking directly at me.

I wriggled about on my chair a bit. His eyes were dark brown and seemed to look right through me.

"I'd been here to see Paul. I'd spent about an hour, maybe more. I'd talked, he'd listened. You know what I'm saying?"

He stopped for a moment and I nodded.

"I thought to myself, it's a week or so since I showed my face to Cooke. I hung around the flats for a while, kept myself out of view. I don't like them to see me, not at first."

"Joey likes to surprise them," Perry said.

"I keep back, in the doorways, round the corners, in the dark. I wait until they're somewhere where I can turn up. So that they know it's just not a coincidence. You know what I'm saying?"

"They never know when he's going to do it," Perry said.

I was listening intently, looking from one to the other as they spoke.

"He came out of the flats and walked straight to Stratford station. He never saw me. He never knew I was there."

"You mean he wasn't following me?" I said, puzzled.

"No. There was no one else around."

"Then why did he go to Oxford Circus?" I said. Joey Hooper didn't seem to be listening.

"I'm on the train and we gets to Oxford Circus." He took a gulp of his tea before continuing. "He's in one carriage and I'm in another. I'm watching through windows, and when he gets off, so do I."

My mind was splitting. One half of me was listening to Joey and the other half was thinking that Kevin Cooke hadn't followed me at all. I'd been wrong about that. He'd arrived at Oxford Circus station independently from me.

"Trouble is there's all these hundreds of people

and I lose him. I'm annoyed. I'm fed up. I go up and down the escalator a couple of times to see if I can see him. I think he's gone, then there's all this commotion. Someone's fell under a train. There's police everywhere. I'm just about to disappear when I see him, standing, a grin on his face, outside the ticket office."

I had an image in my head of the angel-faced Kevin Cooke standing outside the ticket office. It wasn't the picture I wanted at all.

"You didn't see whether he was on the platform when Louise Palmer went under the train?"

"Like I said, I lost him. Oxford Circus is a big station, know what I'm saying?"

"So there's no evidence," I said, glumly. "He was there, but he wasn't there. It won't be enough for the police."

"That's the thing about the Cookes. Nothing sticks to them. They're there, but no one's seen them. They're the invisible men. The night my brother was beaten up nobody was around. One minute Paul was walking home from a night out, the next he's lying in an alley among the rubbish bags. No one saw nothing, not in the street, not in the alley. Five minutes later, no more than five, there's the Cooke brothers and their mate drinking in a pub round the corner."

"Just like at Oxford Circus. Five minutes after she was dead and there he was in front of me," I said.

"I was in the pub, playing snooker. I saw them walk in, the two of them smirking and the other one behind, brushing his jacket down like he's just had some contact with the ground. The three of them buying bottles of lager. You know what I'm saying? Then one of Paul's mates comes running in to find me. There's sirens going. Out on the street there's an ambulance and I see them carrying Paul away. You tell me if that's a coincidence. My brother half dead and those three in the bar two minutes away smirking and acting flash."

"Three of them?" I said.

"Kevin, Lee and Jack. Best buddies. They left my brother for dead on the ground."

"Jack Ross?" I said.

"Jack Ross. Jack Ross who got on the wrong end of Lee Cooke's knife. It broke my heart. Now there's just Kevin to look after."

"But I didn't think that Jack Ross was on friendly terms with the Cookes," I said.

"Sometimes he was. Sometimes he wasn't. It's not my business."

"I thought he was meant to be a nice kid, engaged, going into his dad's building business."

Joey Hooper shrugged. "All I know is that two of them are out of the picture and it just leaves big brother Kev."

"What do you mean?" I said, unsettled by his tone.

Joey Hooper put his hand in his pocket and pulled something out. He bent close to me and under the table opened his palm to show a silver-coloured flick knife. Before I had a second to look around and make sure no one had seen him he pressed a button and a blade shot out.

"Put it away!" I hissed, my eyes glued to the sharpened point.

He carelessly pressed the button again and the blade slid back where it had come from. In a second he had put the knife back into his pocket. I looked at Perry for support, but his eyes were deliberately elsewhere.

"You'll end up in prison!"

"Not me, nope. I'll keep it under control, just like they did."

"If only someone had seen him on the platform!" I said, full of frustration.

If we had just a smidgen of evidence, then Kevin Cooke could be arrested and Joey Hooper wouldn't need to be hanging around corners with a flick knife in his pocket. I made myself look up, avoiding Joey's penetrating stare, around the canteen, into the far corners, at the faces of the other customers, at the notices on the wall. That's when I saw the video camera perched in the corner like a stiff metal bird.

Oxford Circus station would have video cameras. Of course it would! There would be a film of the platform. Why hadn't I thought of it before? I was about to say something when Joey Hooper stood up suddenly, straightening his jeans. I found myself looking at the pocket where the knife was. He saw me and grinned. Then he patted Perry on the head.

"You tell your girlfriend to look after herself, Perry. Know what I'm saying?"

And then he left. Perry gave me a half-smile, almost apologetic.

"Jack Ross beat up Paul Hooper. I never knew that," he said.

"No, neither did I," I said, my attention taken by the camera on the wall.

Could it be that there was an actual picture of Kevin Cooke, on the platform, just before Louise died? I almost crossed my fingers and made a wish.

# 11

# Talking It Through

Sometime later, we dropped Perry off at the end of his street. Billy and I went to the police station to see Heather Warren. Billy was very quiet, but I was buzzing with plans. I had my notebook out on my lap, jotting information down in case I forgot anything.

"I don't know why I didn't think about it!" I said excitedly. "The video cameras. There's every chance that Kevin Cooke might be on them."

"Don't you think the Law will already have looked at the footage? It must be standard procedure to do that when someone falls under a train," Billy said.

I looked around at him in annoyance. His voice sounded tense. Of course I had already thought of that.

"Yes, they'd be looking for footage of the actual victim going off the platform. I'd be looking at the footage of some minutes before, to see if Kevin Cooke was actually there."

"Um."

We sat in silence for a few minutes, joining a long traffic jam in the High Street. Billy took a cigarette out and put it into his mouth. There was tension in the car, like an invisible passenger, sitting between us.

"Is something wrong?" I said, looking at Billy's profile, his mouth tightly shut. "Have I upset you in some way?"

"Your boyfriend rang me up this morning. Wanted to know where you were, what was happening."

"My boyfriend?" I repeated, wondering for a moment who he meant. Then it dawned on me. Brian Martin. He had completely gone out of my head. I cringed inwardly. We'd been seeing each other more or less regularly since the summer and in a day, less than twenty-four hours, I had forgotten about him.

"Oh," I said. I remembered the row about me breaking our Saturday night arrangement, going out on my own.

"Just tell your boyfriend to leave me out of it," Billy said, as we pulled into a parking spot near the police station. "After all," he added in a softer voice, "your love-life's got nothing to do with me."

"I'm sorry. I will," I said. I gathered my stuff

together and, feeling altogether less buoyant than before, got out of the car.

Heather Warren looked pleased to see us. We sat down in her office while she finished filing some papers.

"I'll just get these out of the way – I won't be a minute." She had a pen sticking out the side of her mouth like a cigar. I wondered if she had finally managed to give up smoking.

She was kneeling down at the bottom drawer of a filing cabinet. I noticed she was wearing pinstriped trousers and that a matching jacket was hanging over the back of her chair. Her hair was much shorter than I'd seen it before and she'd had it coloured a dramatic auburn red. I liked it.

I'd known Heather since I'd started working in my uncle's agency. She was an able woman who'd been promoted above the men in her office and it had upset a few people. My uncle Tony didn't like her. He called her a *feminist* as though it were an insult. Over the previous eighteen months she'd helped me on some of my cases, even though she wasn't always pleased to see me. I admired her. She was bright and got things done. She liked me, but she thought I was just playing at being a detective and had tried on numerous occasions to get me to join the police force. I hadn't seen her since the summer.

"Are you involved with the Jack Ross stabbing?" I said nervously, after we'd exchanged a few pleasantries. I knew, from the past, that she was quite likely to be annoyed that I hadn't contacted the police as soon as Louise Palmer had got in touch with me.

"Not personally," she said, tidying things up on her desk. "Have you got something for us?" She looked hard at me, her eyes narrowed. I could see, for the first time, how disconcerting it might be to be interrogated by her.

"I think so," I said, feeling my confidence crumble a little. "I should have come before really..." I carried on. Out of the blue, I felt Billy's hand on my arm, steadying it.

"Start at the beginning, Patsy," he said, his voice soothing. I took a deep breath and told the story.

Heather had got us all a cup of coffee. Mine was too strong but I didn't say anything, I just sipped it gingerly. She was on the phone to the detective who'd been in charge of the case. Billy was drinking his down in great mouthfuls. I could hear Heather saying, *Um ... um ... yes ... um ... I know ... that's what I thought ... it's a possibility, though ... it's worth looking into ... um ... um.*

"OK." She replaced the receiver with a bang. "That was Des Murray, he's working the case. I think you know him, don't you, Patsy?"

I nodded glumly.

"He's very annoyed that you didn't come forward straight away last night. That was naughty of you, Patsy. You know how important it is for us to have all the facts."

I didn't say anything. There were no excuses that I could make.

"They've looked through the video footage of the accident but it's inconclusive. Des Murray isn't thrilled about you coming in to look at the tapes, but if you make a statement about your conversation with Louise Palmer that should calm him. Careful though, don't tread on his toes. You know what a chauvinist he is!"

"What about Lee Cooke? Is he still in prison?" I said, changing the subject slightly.

"Yes, there's a hearing later this week. It may well be that the lawyer gets all the charges dropped because of lack of evidence. We've still got Louise Palmer's original statement, but without her to back it up the case won't go much further."

"Would I be able to see that statement?" I said.

"I doubt that Des Murray will allow that." She was beginning to sound peeved.

"I was acting on behalf of Louise's mother, Heather. I wasn't just interfering. She was the one who told me not to involve the police. She knew that it would scare Louise off."

"I know that, Patsy, but like I've said in the past,

we are trained for this job and you're not and no matter how well meaning you are, you simply can't do it the way we can."

"That's not fair. Patsy's handled things well enough in the past. If it wasn't for her I'd still be in prison," Billy said briskly, as if he were making a complaint in a shop.

"She's worked hard, I can't deny it, but she's been lucky. Even she would admit that." Heather looked at me.

"I'm here now," I said, interrupting, wanting to move on from the argument.

"It's a start," Heather said with a sigh. She took a quick look at her watch. A microsecond, no more, but I guessed that it was time to wind up.

"What about the Hooper brothers? Will you be able to look into the attack on Paul Hooper? He's still lying in a coma in the London Hospital."

"It's out of my area, but I know someone over in Highbury. I'll ask a few questions, see if I can find anything out. I'm not promising anything."

We all stood up then and I turned towards the door of her office. She was saying something to Billy, but I didn't catch what it was because Joey Hooper and his flick knife had come into my mind. It was the one detail that I'd not told Heather. The knife had shocked me. It had only sat there for a second or two: eight or ten centimetres long, cold stainless steel, it had flicked out like magic. Now you see it, now you don't. How long, I wondered, before Joey Hooper got fed up following Kevin Cooke and decided to use it?

It was almost seven o'clock by the time we drove into my street. A fine drizzle had started, hardly enough to merit using the wipers. The streetlights were yellow and fuzzy round the edges. Cars were parked bumper to bumper and we had to drive along a way before we found a space. Billy was more talkative than before.

"When are you going to see Mrs Palmer?"

"Tomorrow. After I look at the videotapes." I wasn't looking forward to it.

Billy clicked off the ignition and the lights. All at once there was a hush inside the car. Some young boys were leaning against a garden wall across the way, two of them on bikes, the others just standing. I could see pinpricks of cigarettes in the dark.

We sat there for a few minutes not saying anything. It was a comfortable silence, neither of us feeling the need to talk. The kids across the street were laughing uproariously about something and didn't seem to notice the fine spray of rain that was hitting them. I could see it in the beam of light from the street lamp. Two of the boys were black and three were white. One white kid had his arm round one of the black kids' shoulders and was whispering something to him, after which more laughter spilled out.

I started to think about the Cooke brothers and the racist attitudes that had led them to go and beat up Paul Hooper. Riverside Boys' school had a reputation for trouble of that sort; the whites against the blacks, the whites against the Asians, the whites against the Turkish or Chinese.

My school was different. I honestly didn't remember white and black kids not getting on with each other. Me and Billy, we had black friends. Lots of them.

Don't get me wrong, I'm not saying there wasn't racism. During the time I was there, several black kids were beaten up by some boys from a nearby school who waited for them to pass through a stretch of parkland, before they pounced on them. Then there was a huge fuss when a group calling themselves The British Party hired the school hall for a meeting. I was at the demonstration with my mum and my classmates and lots of local ethnic groups. Their posters were frightening. *Britain for the whites!* they screamed, and we all chanted loudly every time someone tried to go through the school gates. They had to call the meeting off in the end.

Then there was the house that got burned down two streets away from Billy. An Asian man and his wife and four small children lived there. One of my classmates was related to the wife, a cousin or something, I think. In the middle of the night someone, some brave person, stuffed a rag soaked with petrol through their letterbox. It smouldered for hours before igniting powerfully and leaping up the stairs. I knew about fires, I was nearly killed by one not so long before. The family woke up and had to get out of the upstairs bedroom window and jump. Luckily the front garden was overgrown; long grass and bushes broke the fall of most of the family. One little boy didn't make it, though. They got him out but he'd inhaled a lot of smoke and died in the ambulance on the way to hospital. That was what the arsonist had achieved. He'd killed a four-year-old Asian boy. Very courageous.

In class, though, among the people me and Billy hung around with, there wasn't any tension.

"I don't remember any racism among our crowd, when we were at school," I said to Billy, breaking the long silence.

"That's because you're not black," Billy said.

"What do you mean?"

"You weren't the focus of any attacks or abuse, so you don't remember it."

"But who was? Out of the kids in our class, I mean?"

"Shirley Miller had the words *blacks go home* painted over her locker! Remember the mouthful she gave to the boys who did it!"

"Well..."

"Peter Prince, remember him? He had several rucks in the playground over name-calling. And the

Sikh kids, Gurvinder and Rajesh? The names they got called! You must remember the meeting they arranged when all the Sikh kids went to see the headteacher with a list of demands."

"I don't remember," I said.

"No, because it didn't affect you. That's why."

It was true. What he said was right. I had black friends and I told kids off if I heard anyone making what I thought was a racist comment, but I didn't feel the hurt of it. I didn't suffer the actual humiliation.

"When I was in prison, a young African boy was in the next cell," Billy said. "He was originally from Somalia and he came over to this country to get away from a war and one thing and another got in with a bad crowd. Ended up on remand, waiting for more than six months. On the third day I was there, he got beaten up by three white guys. They said he was sucking up to the guards, but I think it was just that they were fed up and he looked different, spoke with an accent and ate different food."

The car seemed even quieter as Billy spoke. Only the patter of the rain sounded. The boys who'd been standing around had gone and the street around us was dark and still.

"They got him in the toilets. They'd roughed him up a bit and the word went round, and out of the blue these five Afro-Caribbean kids turned up. No one knew exactly where they'd come from, which wing, which section. They just marched into the toilets. They stood at the door and wouldn't let the white kids out until they apologized to the Somali boy. There were five of them see and they looked like they could handle themselves."

Billy was shaking his head and I didn't know what to say. My throat was dry and hard and I reached out a hand and grabbed his arm.

"I tried to go for the guards, so that they would stop it but one of the black kids said, *Leave it, we fight our own battles*. Eventually the white kids came out, walking along the walkway back to their own cells. Someone, I'm not sure who, started a slow handclap. It was weird, like a drum. I was unnerved by it all, by the hatred of the whites, by the hardness of the black kids."

He shook his head and closed his eyes.

It was horrible. I had no idea what kind of pain and humiliation people had to suffer. I was a white girl brought up in a comfortable home and had never faced these things. I moved across and put my arm around Billy. A few seconds passed and then he turned his body towards me and hugged me tightly.

A few moments later, Billy's head was still on my shoulder and with my free hand I was patting and stroking his hair. I could smell the smoke from him and feel the warmth of his chest and neck. Behind him I could see the window, glistening by then with raindrops. As I watched the water skid across the glass, a vague longing was stirring inside me. I felt Billy's breath on my cheek and turned my head from side to side gently, his skin rubbing against mine. His arms were gripping me and one hand was holding on to my shoulder-blade tightly.

I pulled my head back a few centimetres and kissed him. Slowly at first; my mouth just touching his. For a few moments he didn't respond, just stayed still, his hand still gripping my arm. I went ahead, though, pushing my lips up to his and turning my head from side to side. His mouth opened slowly, as if he wasn't sure it was what he wanted to do, and his fingers climbed nervously up my neck and into my hair.

It had been so long since we kissed or held each other. I didn't want it to stop. Pausing for breath, I opened my eyes and looked over Billy's shoulder. The driver's window was partially misted up and through it there was the vague shape of a figure standing leaning against the wall where the young boys had been. I closed my eyes again and could feel Billy's mouth on my neck, sending tingling sensations across my shoulders.

"We can't keep meeting like this." I heard Billy's voice trying to make light of it.

I smiled and opened my eyes and was about to speak, to say something, when I began to focus on the figure who was leaning so casually against the wall in the pouring rain. A thin finger of worry began to niggle at my insides and with my free hand I reached across and wiped the steamed-up window clear.

My heart dipped and I sat back, disengaging myself from Billy.

"Oh no," I said.

"What's the matter?" Billy's voice was soft and anxious.

"It's Brian Martin," I said. "He's standing out in the rain, watching us."

Brian Martin waited until I got out of the car. He stood in the rain while I picked up my stuff out of the back seat and steeled myself to face him. He let me close the car door and walk across the road towards him, the rain like tiny darts hitting me at every step.

He let me get within a metre of him. Close enough to see the hurt on his face, his mouth tightly shut as though he was afraid of what might come out of it.

"Brian, I'm sorry," I said. What else could I say?

Without a word he just turned and walked away up the street.

# 12
# Video

The next morning I watched the video footage in a frosty silence. Des Murray was standing behind me, his presence exuding annoyance. His fingers were tapping on the back of my chair and a long ribbon of smoke curled over my shoulder and disappeared into the air. I coughed loudly and moved around in my chair hoping he would go away but he didn't.

I held the remote in my hand and clicked on the fast forward button, looking at the time on the top left-hand side of the screen. When I got to 19:50, I slowed down and let the pictures run at normal speed. The video I was watching was from the far end of the platform, from behind where Louise had got off the train and walked towards me. I'd been right down the other end just as she'd got off. That's when I'd walked forward, tentatively, waiting to see if it was her.

The image in front of me was vague. I could make out dark figures on the screen, many of them, but I couldn't single out anyone in particular. I watched for a few minutes while a train pulled in.

"This is the train she was on, we think," Des Murray said, grudgingly.

I couldn't see any detail. Just dark figures crowding together around the doors and others squeezing through to get off.

"Is this all there is?" I said.

In my head there was a perfect picture of what had happened. It was like a film that you'd see in a cinema. The train pulls in, the doors open and Louise Palmer gets off. A close-up of her face then, her head turning this way and that, looking down the platform for me. A shot of me leaning against the wall, my eyes recognizing Louise, standing alertly, walking slowly forward to meet her. The red balloon floats in front of me and bars my view of Louise. The camera cuts to the train in the tunnel then back to Louise, who smiles and starts to walk towards me. A whole gang of teenagers spill on to the platform between us and look up at the red balloon. A close-up of Louise's face, smiling at me. Then her expression changes to one of fear. She turns and runs. The camera shows a close-up of me, looking at the red balloon then at Louise, then it shifts and a face is seen over my shoulder. That face is Kevin Cooke's. He ducks out of sight and seconds later the train comes in and there's a terrible screaming sound.

"Don't these things ever do close-ups?" I said, looking grumpily at Des Murray.

"They're worked from a central office. The operator will only zoom in if something looks odd. The other video shows the escaped balloon. You get a better picture on it."

"Can I see it?" I said, as politely as I could.

He took a long deep breath, inhaling enough air to lift him off the ground. I smiled nicely and watched as he went over to a desk and sorted through a drawer.

Des Murray had been involved on a case that I was on almost a year before. He was about thirty, not what you'd call happy in his job. He hadn't liked my involvement then and I could see he wasn't exactly overjoyed to see me now. I ignored it, took the tape off him and put it into the machine. I ran it forward until the time showed 19:50 again.

This time the angle was different. The camera must have been at the other end, near where I was standing. I watched for a few minutes and saw the young students piling on to the platform. Although I couldn't see Louise Palmer, I knew that at that point she was probably about twenty metres away. A second later, everyone was looking up in the air and the camera swept back and forth and then zoomed in. I couldn't see the balloon on the screen, only the upturned faces of the passengers. At the far edge of the picture I saw Louise Palmer join the edge of the crowd and smile. I remembered that look. I was off screen somewhere, feeling pleased with myself that she'd turned up. The camera zoomed in a bit further on her part of the crowd, then it swung away in a half circle and was focusing on the group that I was among. I could see the corner of my hat at the side of someone's head. I looked hard. There were about three or four faces around me, a couple directly behind. I squinted my eyes to see, but it was too indistinct. Disappointment settled on me.

"These pictures are too small," I said to Des Murray. "How can you tell anything from them?"

"What's there to tell? There was a distraction along the platform. Everyone was looking up, as well as the Palmer girl. It was crowded, the kid took a wrong footing. It's a shame. Nice-looking girl like that."

It was my turn to take a slow deep breath. I honestly did dislike Des Murray. *Nice-looking girl.* What if she hadn't been a nice-looking girl?

I looked back at the screen. What I really needed was to get some stills from the video blown up. That was probably costly, though, and it wouldn't be something that Des Murray would want to do. I sat back for a few minutes.

"I wonder if…" I said, looking hard at the screen and then at Des Murray. "I wonder if these could be enlarged? No … you probably couldn't sanction it. I'd probably have to speak to whoever's in charge of the case," I said. I was tapping my forefinger against my lip and looking as though I was thinking hard.

"I'm in charge of the case," Des Murray said.

"Oh, I know," I said, turning to face him. "I know you are, but I was thinking that to get these enlarged, you'd need to get permission from London Transport and stuff, you'd have to speak to the person like in overall charge, you know, above you."

"I'm in charge of the case," he repeated, firmly.

"Yes, of course. Everyday stuff. But I was thinking of decisions, like big decisions."

"That's me. M.E. I make the decisions."

"Oh," I said.

"Why do you keep going on about having them enlarged?" he said sulkily.

"I was there, Des. I saw her face. She definitely saw someone she knew apart from me. I thought if you got the pictures enlarged we could look. Just so that we don't leave any stone unturned."

He was quiet for a minute, looking hard at the screen.

"I could ask Heather for permission if you like."

"I don't need permission from anybody. I make my own decisions!"

I stood up and walked towards the door, giving

him space. His face was blank, but he must have been thinking it through because he said, "We'll get them enlarged. See what's there. You can see them when they're ready."

"Oh thanks, Des," I said, giving a sweet little-girl smile. Sometimes you just have to use every tool you've got.

"Couple of days. I'll be in touch." He said it gruffly and turned away to pick up the phone.

I crept out of the office, smiling to myself. Sometimes, even when it looked impossible, things went right.

The feelgood factor left me as soon as I stepped out of the police station and walked along the street. It was a dull day, not grey so much as browny. The trees had been stripped of their leaves, their branches naked and thin, reaching forlornly into the sky. Scattered across the pavements, lying among the discarded drink cans and empty crisp packets, were the damp brown and yellow leaves. They lay still on the ground like hundreds of palm prints.

I had to go and visit Mrs Palmer. In my bag I had the photos of Louise that I had borrowed. I thought they would probably be important to her and I was going to return them.

It wasn't raining, but the sky looked spongy and people were holding umbrellas at half-mast, looking cagily up from time to time, in case the downpour caught them unawares. I walked quickly in the direction of the estate and let myself think about Brian Martin.

I'd been downright unkind to him. He and I had got together when Billy had been sent to prison. At the time he'd said to me, "When Billy Rogers comes out you won't want to see me again!" I'd denied it, sure that it wouldn't happen. I was wrong, though. I had tired of him. Instead of doing the right thing, telling him that it was over, I had left him to discover it for himself. I felt like a real rat.

But then there was Billy Rogers and me and this invisible pull between us. This time it had been me who had recklessly started it all off. I remembered the way he had slid his finger behind my ear and along my neck, making one long shiver run down to my chest. In the past, embarrassment would usually have made us gloss it over, pretend it hadn't happened. This time, though, I was determined not to let it drop. Something good had to come out of it, especially after having treated Brian Martin so badly.

I only spent a short time with Mrs Palmer. She had several people in her tiny flat; Mr and Mrs Ross were there with Frank, as well as a couple of neighbours. I couldn't manage to say all the things I wanted, so I just asked about the funeral and said I'd definitely be there. The rest of the time I sat quietly and listened sympathetically.

Mrs Palmer seemed a bit distracted, running round getting small glasses of sickly, sweet sherry for everyone. I wondered, for a brief moment, whether she actually remembered who I was. It didn't matter. I was only grateful that she hadn't decided to tell me off, blame me for not bringing Louise back.

I noticed, as time went on, that Frank Ross hadn't touched his sherry. He looked as formal as when I'd seen him before, only this time he was wearing a light grey suit and maroon tie. He was fidgeting with a substantial-looking umbrella and now and then he glanced, for just a minisecond, at his watch. When he got up to leave, I decided to go as well. I hoped I'd be able to have a chat with him.

I gulped down the last of the sherry and followed along the hallway as Mrs Palmer let us out.

"Thanks for coming, Frank," she said, giving him a hug and kiss. Her voice sounded slightly slurred, as if she'd had too many glasses of sherry.

"Are you sure you don't need us over the next couple of days?" Frank Ross said. "Only you know I said I'd take Mum and Dad to Clacton to see our gran. Truth is, she's really ill and they haven't even told her about Jack yet. God knows what she'll say when she hears about Louise as well."

"No, no, you go. It'll do your mum and dad good to get away for a few days. As long as you're back for the funeral on Friday. That's all I care. Just be there when I bury my Louise."

"We will. We're coming back early Friday morning. Look after yourself."

He walked out of the door and I said a hurried goodbye to Mrs Palmer, intent on catching up with him. She held me back, though, telling me yet again the arrangements for the funeral.

"It's at St Peter's. A lovely church in Bethnal Green. Not that we were churchgoers, but still... Ten o'clock. Don't be late, my dear."

"I won't," I said, about to leave and follow Frank Ross. I paused, though, as a glassy tear emerged from her eye and her tiny hand rested on my arm like a nervous bird.

"She had everything in front of her, my Louise. Her whole life. I just don't understand how she could have fallen like that..."

She looked ravaged, the lines around her eyes looking stark in the daylight. I felt so sorry for her, but there was nothing I could do or say that would make her feel any better. I squeezed her hand for a moment and then turned and left.

When I heard the front door close behind me, I made a little run so that I could catch up with Frank Ross, who was walking briskly ahead.

"Hang on," I said. "Mind if I walk with you?"

"Free country," he said, with a half-smile. He was using his umbrella as though it was a walking stick.

"Only I wanted to ask you a couple of things."

"Fire away," he said, continuing to walk as though he was in a race.

"I was under the impression, from what the

police and Louise said, that your brother was a bitter enemy of the Cooke brothers."

"So?"

"But I've also heard that he and the Cookes were friends. Got involved in some stuff together. Like when Paul Hooper got beaten up. I heard that your brother was with Lee and Kevin when that happened." I was puffing my words out trying to keep up with him.

He stopped abruptly and I almost walked on past him.

"Just because my brother and I looked alike, everyone thought that we were the same. That we liked the same things, went to the same places, had the same friends. We were different, though. I work in a solicitor's. I don't spend my time hanging around with lowlife like the Cookes. My brother had his own life. Don't ask me to tell you about it."

"It's just that if he was friends with the Cookes, it seems funny that one of them should have killed him," I said.

"What's it got to do with you anyway?" he said, looking straight at me. There was a cold look to his eyes.

"Excuse me, but Mrs Palmer asked me to help her find Louise." I said it defensively.

"Well, excuse me, but you didn't do a very good job of it!"

And he walked off. Leaving me standing on the

pavement. I looked around with embarrassment, imagining that everyone on the street had seen him walking away from me. I gave a couple of little coughs then bent down to tie up my shoelace, pausing long enough for anyone to pass by. Raindrops appeared around me on the pavement like splashes of paint, and I stood up and pulled my collar up round my neck. In seconds there was a downpour, nothing short of a monsoon. I pulled open my rucksack to get my umbrella out and felt the photographs of Louise still there. I was immediately annoyed with myself. I'd meant to give them back to Mrs Palmer.

I found a shop doorway to stand in until it dried up, and looked at the two photographs again.

The dancing school group; JINGLES DANCE STUDIO, *Louise Palmer, Lisa Black, Sherry Stevens, freestyle presentation, May.* Pretty girls, serious and sombre-looking, their bodies in different poses, looking as though they were going to break into some modern dance routine. Then the photo of Jack Ross and Louise, sitting on a settee, Jack Ross smiling slyly, looking the exact double of his brother Frank who had just walked off on me. *My brother had his own life. Don't ask me to tell you about it.* Louise Palmer giving a model-girl smile. *She had everything in front of her, my Louise.*

The happy couple. Now they were both dead.

# 13

# New Technology

My uncle was in the office when I got there in the early afternoon. He asked me how I'd got on at the doctor's and I hesitated for a minute before I remembered that I'd asked my mum to ring up and make an excuse for me.

"Fine," I said. "Had to wait awhile, that's why I'm so late."

"Only I've got to go to lunch," he said, picking his jacket up and hugging it to him. "Nothing wrong then? At the doctor's?"

"No, just..." I hesitated, not sure of what my mum had said. "Just women's trouble."

"Oh." He nodded his head rapidly, his eyes looking down at the floor, over at the computer, up at the ceiling. *Women's trouble*. Why did it embarrass him? He had a wife and a daughter!

"Have you lost any weight?" I said, to break the tension.

"Two pounds. Just over two pounds." He smiled and patted his stomach.

"That's good."

"Just cutting out the unnecessaries," he said, glancing over at the cupboard where we kept the tea and coffee things, the pink wafer biscuits and the Hobnobs.

"Well done," I said. I actually thought that biscuits were one of life's necessities.

"I haven't missed them," he said, with a sigh that suggested otherwise. He put his jacket on and picked up his case and keys.

"Will you be long?" I said. I knew he was going out to look for new business again.

"Most of the afternoon, I should think," he said. "I'll pop into M&S and get a low-calorie sandwich and some mineral water. Then I'm off to Blacks to see if they have anything for us. I may also call into the solicitor's. If things don't look up soon, Patricia, I don't quite know what we'll do."

Blacks was the insurance company that Tony had done business with for years. Just lately the work seemed to have dried up, though. Had the world become honest? I didn't know, but I was willing to bet that it hadn't.

As soon as he left I put the kettle on and looked in the tray on my desk to see what there was for me to do. A couple of phone calls chasing up old overdue accounts, some letters to type to old clients of Tony's and introductory letters to run off on the computer and send out to prospective clients, other insurance companies, large department stores and solicitors. I groaned. I'd been doing this kind of stuff for weeks and nothing had come of it. *Dear Sir, May I introduce you to the services of our agency? Superior investigative skills at your disposal. Our highly trained operatives will pursue any inquiry until its conclusion…* It all sounded too much like an official letter from the Queen. It smacked of old English black and white films and men in deerstalkers with close friends called Dr Watson. If we had had an address in Mayfair it might have worked, been amusing even. But with an East End postcode it just didn't fit.

I decided to play around for a while. I made a new heading with the agency's name, **Anthony Hamer Investigations Inc** using a modern bold font. Underneath I typed **Associate Patsy Kelly**. Then I put in big letters, "Working Against Crime In East London". I smiled at what it looked like and went on to compose the leaflet: *Here, in East London, the agency has been at the forefront of private detection work. Whether working with the police or on our own. No case is too trivial. No investigation too large. We use the latest in computer technology and have highly developed surveillance techniques. Male and female* *consultants. Totally confidential.* Underneath, in a variety of fonts and sizes I listed the kinds of work the agency did. Then I printed it all off.

It looked brilliant, but I knew that Tony wouldn't like it.

I hesitated for a minute and then printed off twenty copies. I opened the Yellow Pages and looked through for the names of big companies, transport firms, the local water and electricity companies, large superstores, anything that caught my eye. I put them all in envelopes and stuck second-class stamps on them. Then I saved the file on the computer and went out of the office down to the post box on the corner and slipped them all in. There was every chance that we'd never hear from any of them. And if we did? I'd explain about the new letter then.

When I got back to the office I saw that it was only twenty to three. I sat down in front of the computer and thought about Louise Palmer and her case that seemed to be complicated and vague at the same time. In front of me the screen was black, with dozens of coloured windows appearing like planets moving towards me. When I touched the mouse they disappeared and I was faced with the blank screen of the computer, like the first page of a new exercise book just waiting for me to write something on it.

I was reminded for an instant of the days in

school when I'd written on the last page of a dog-eared exercise book and the teacher was forced into giving me a new one. It sat thick and solid in the middle of my desk like a new beginning. The previous book was graffitied, curly at the edges, full of my attempts to get things right, the teacher's red ticks and curt comments: *Is this all? Take care with your presentation, Paragraphs please, Spelling!* The new book was a chance to turn over a new leaf. I remembered how much care I would take over the very first piece of work, making sure there were no mistakes. The fresh book was symbolic; a chance to start over.

I looked at the computer screen and several ideas came together inside my head. I got up and went to the cupboard for a new disk. I got a sticky label and wrote the word PALMER on it and put the disk into the computer. I pressed NEW for a new file, a fresh page, a brand spanking new book. At the top I wrote the date, *Monday 18th November*. Then I spent about thirty minutes typing every single detail that I could remember about the case on to the screen. Tipping out my rucksack, I scanned over my notebook and typed out a list of names, places, dates on to the screen.

Then I sat back and redrafted it, adding and changing bits that weren't quite right. I filled six pages of the file. Six pages! In school I'd always found it difficult to write anything more than a couple of sides on any subject. That's why my A-levels had been such a slog. I added a couple of lines to the end about the day and place of the funeral, *Friday 10 o'clock, St Peter's, Bethnal Green.* I read over it a couple of times and found certain bits sticking out, staying in my mind after I'd finished. I decided then to use one of the classic note-taking skills that I'd learned in school. *Pull out the main points of the material.*

1. Jack Ross is stabbed on Bonfire Night outside Wood Road Park.
2. His girlfriend Louise Palmer identifies the attacker as Lee Cooke, who is later arrested by the police.
3. Kevin Cooke, Lee's brother, threatens Louise Palmer so she runs away.
4. She stays with her friend Sherry Stevens, who she knew from Jingles.
5. She agrees to meet me at Oxford Circus and come back in for police protection.
6. Louise Palmer falls under a Central Line train.
7. Kevin Cooke is most certainly there at the time.
8. There is video footage, but it doesn't show much.
9. The Cooke brothers and Jack Ross are supposedly enemies, but earlier the three of them beat up Paul Hooper in a racist attack and left him in a coma.
10. His brother, Joey Hooper, stalks Kevin Cooke and carries a knife in his pocket.

Then I turned to the list of names I'd typed. I'd put down every single one that I could think of that had come up in the case.

Louise Palmer, Lee and Kevin Cooke, Jack and Frank Ross, Paul and Joey Hooper, Sherry Stevens, Lisa Black. I jumbled them about and put each into a different font. I also centred Louise Palmer's name and made it bigger than the rest. I sat back and looked at the page. Lee Cooke's name was in small bold letters. Kevin Cooke's name had come out in a kind of Gothic print that looked a bit ghostly. Jack Ross's name had appeared in tall thin letters that suggested elegance and his brother Frank was in a squat, heavy font. That's the wrong way round, I thought, remembering Frank Ross and his posh suits and rolled-up umbrella. Sherry Stevens and Lisa Black were in italics so that the letters were all slanted to the right. You could almost imagine a row of dancers swaying together.

I pressed PRINT and waited while the machine made a smooth whirring sound and watched as the paper unrolled out of the printer. I was pleased with it all. I read it over again, being impressed with my own memory and notes. It was solid and thorough and I was sure I hadn't left anything out.

Taking a highlighter pen from the drawer, I decided to mark the most obvious factors. Over and over I found the name Kevin Cooke standing out in fluorescent blue. He had threatened Louise. He was at the station. He had every reason to stop her coming back into the police. He had even followed me that morning in the hope of tracking Louise down.

I stopped highlighting and thought for a minute. Joey Hooper had said that on the Saturday evening Kevin Cooke hadn't been following me. So how did he know that Louise was going to be there?

Someone must have *told* him.

I looked over my notes again. The fourth point I had made said, *She stays with her friend Sherry Stevens*. Where did Louise go after she left Sherry's house? What had happened to her in those hours between leaving Sherry's and attempting to meet me at Oxford Circus?

Something else occurred to me. When Louise had phoned me on the mobile, she asked me if I'd heard about her mum's flat being attacked. How had she known that? Nobody, not even her mother, knew where she was. Perhaps she had rung someone on the estate, someone that she confided in. Could that person have told Kevin Cooke when and where she was meeting me?

I squared off the pages and stapled them together. I'd been silly. I should have *started* the investigation by finding out what Louise had done between the time she left Sherry's house and the time I was supposed to meet her on the station. I'd been too bogged down in trying to prove Kevin Cooke's presence on the platform.

It was a good place to make a fresh start on the investigation. I felt positive and pulled out my notes. A quick phone call to Sherry Stevens' home told me that she was at Jingles rehearsing and she would be there all afternoon and part of the evening. I got out my AtoZ and looked up the address.

# 14
# Jingles

I had two skirts on the bed to choose from. One was black silk with purple flowers on it and it came down to my ankles. I'd bought it recently from a stall down at the market. The other was a short yellow and black tartan kilt that I'd picked up at a charity shop. Either way I'd be wearing thick tights and boots under them and my zip-up leather jacket on top. I had also picked a small wool pillbox hat that had embroidery over it. It was something my mum had bought me from a holiday in Morocco some years before.

I'd already put some make-up on and brushed my hair up into a high ponytail, twisting it under so that it looked like a bun and would fit nicely under the hat. All I had to do was decide between the two skirts.

Don't get me wrong, I don't spend hours thinking about clothes or how I look. I'm pretty ordinary on the whole; average height, weight, hair colour, no distinguishing marks. I don't spend a fortune on clothes and I shop mainly for comfort. I couldn't spend hard-earned money on something that was short and tight that meant I couldn't bend over or go up stairs without worrying which parts of my anatomy were on show. I like loose clothes, things that layer one on top of the other. I like wearing floaty things with heavy jumpers and boots and socks and I often wear my jeans with an old lace or chiffon top. I like mixing things. It gives off odd signals, makes it hard for people to sum me up.

I put my DMs on and looked at the skirts again.

Sherry Stevens had been a confident, strident person, who had made me look foolish. When I saw her again I wanted to make a better impression. I picked up the tartan kilt. It looked solid but off-beat at the same time, especially if I wore the black leather with it.

I wasn't sure. Earlier I'd phoned Billy and asked him to pick me up at the dance studio. The prospect of seeing him had made me feel the tiniest bit excited. I sat down on the bed and ran my fingers across the silk skirt. I imagined it flowing around my legs. It had been ages since Billy had seen me in anything other than jeans. I picked it up, about to undo the zip when Brian Martin's face came into my head. A feeling of guilt, like a bag of cement, settled in my stomach.

I threw the silk skirt aside and picked up the kilt and put it on.

The dance studio was in Spitalfields. I took a bus that got me there in about fifteen minutes. The address was up a pedestrian street and down an alley. It looked like some kind of old warehouse that had been renovated. Outside, the word JINGLES sat on the wall in neon strip-lighting. That was all. It could have been a restaurant, a clothes shop or a hairdresser's. Inside, it was all smoked glass and pictures of dancers in clip frames. Several young girls walked past me wearing a variety of leotards and trainers; some had pumps or ballet shoes on. There was no reception area, just settees and a line of TV monitors, which showed different dance studios in operation. A couple of them were doing keep-fit stuff, lines of young women marching on the spot, stretching their arms to some musical beat that I couldn't hear. One of the studios had a ballet class and in another there seemed to be some kind of Asian dancing, women in saris moving around in slow circles. The last monitor showed a theatre area with a stage; there was a production going on, a scene that the dancers were trying over and over. I wondered if that was what Sherry was involved in.

"Can I help you?" a voice came from behind me.

"I'm looking for Sherry Stevens," I said, looking at a tall, tanned woman in a pink floral dressing gown. Her hair was flattened to her head and covered with a tight nylon cap. In her hand she was twirling a blonde wig. She was glowing faintly with sweat, breathing deeply as though she'd been in a long run a while before.

"Sherry should be out soon. There's a break in the rehearsal coming up. I'll tell her someone's waiting. Why don't you take a seat?"

"Thanks," I said and watched as she walked away, her feet only lightly coming into contact with the ground before she disappeared inside a red security door. I wandered across to a display noticeboard which was covered in pictures of dancers, mostly in costume, and listings of the classes held. I found myself looking along the lists of Modern Dancing, Sequence Dancing, Belly Dancing and wondered if I could build up the courage to take a class. At the side was an advert for the Christmas production of *East Side Story, a story of love in a time of racial tension, set in the East End of London*. Across the middle of it was a sticker that said FULL DRESS REHEARSAL FRIDAY 22ND NOV 4 O'CLOCK. I was about to read on when I saw a woman with short blonde hair came out of the red door and walk towards me. I looked up quizzically and only after a couple of seconds did I realize that it was Sherry Stevens. She pulled a blonde wig off and grimaced at me.

"What are you doing here?" she said, using her fingers to scratch at her scalp and shake her own dark hair that had been flattened under the wig.

"I need to ask you a couple of things," I said.

"I've spoken to the police. I'm not going to go over it all again to you."

"Please. It will only take a couple of minutes."

"Patsy Kelly, that is your name, isn't it? If you hadn't interfered Louise might still be alive now."

"How do you work that one out?" I said, my anger bubbling up.

"She was all right at my place. She was safe there."

"Perhaps if you'd been honest with me, and not led me halfway across London, she might still be all right," I said, raising my voice louder than I meant to. It was faulty logic, but I said it anyway. She gave a long-suffering sigh.

"What do you want to know, Patsy? I've only got a couple of minutes break before I'm back on." She rolled her eyes and I had to control my temper.

A couple of passing dancers in wigs looked at us and said hi to Sherry.

"I just need to know where Louise went after she left your flat on Saturday."

"I've been through all this with the police, Patsy," she said, with great patience, running her fingers over the wig, teasing clumps of hair out.

"I'm just asking for a bit of help here, Sherry.

After leading me astray on Saturday, don't you at least owe me that?"

"She went to Lisa Black's flat."

"I thought she'd moved to Devon?"

"Wrong again. Her family moved to Devon. She stayed in London."

"Address?" I said curtly, trying not to rise to the constant sarcasm in her tone.

A woman's voice popped out of the security door. Sherry snatched my pen from me and began writing on the back of a nearby leaflet.

"You're on, Sherry!" the woman said and then disappeared.

She handed the paper to me and said, her voice softer than before, "Lisa won't be able to tell you anything. Louise only stayed there for a couple of hours. After that, who knows?" She shrugged her shoulders and started to put the wig back on, her hands cupping over her ears as she did it. I looked down at the paper: *20, Park Road, Whitechapel.*

Then she disappeared behind the door without so much as a goodbye.

I'd only met Sherry Stevens twice and both times I ended up feeling at a disadvantage. I stood back and looked up at the monitor where the rehearsal was going on. A few seconds later, Sherry walked on to the stage area and joined half a dozen other girls in blonde wigs. They all began warming up and I watched as Sherry did several ballet exercises. Then

I zipped my leather jacket up and went outside to wait for Billy.

He drove up a few moments later and I was immediately disappointed to see that Perry was in the back of the car. I had hoped that he would come alone and that we could talk about the previous evening.

"All right, Patsy? You going Scottish dancing?" Perry said and chortled.

I looked down at the yellow and black kilt and wished I hadn't worn it. The long silk skirt would have been better, made me look a bit more classy.

"What's it to you?" I said, getting into the passenger's seat.

"How'd you get on?" Billy said, pulling out from the pavement before I had a chance to look him straight in the face.

"Fine," I said, looking at Lisa Black's address. "I got what I wanted."

Or had I? I wasn't sure and didn't feel like talking about it.

# 15

# Love and Redundancy

After a restless night I decided to do some things before I went to work. Lisa Black couldn't see me until about ten, so I went to Billy's first. I left a message for Tony on the answer-phone to say I was pricing up photocopiers for the agency. I didn't think he would mind.

The sun was squeezing in and out between heavy clouds; dull one minute, hot the next. I'd put my leather jacket on, but it was too warm, so I carried it over my arm.

Billy's garage doors were open, so I didn't bother knocking. When I went in I saw him leaning against the brick wall, a cigarette in his hand, looking at a Jaguar car that he had bought some months before.

He was wearing jeans and a T-shirt and nothing on his feet. Even though it wasn't cold outside he looked underdressed. He saw me and gave a half-smile.

"I'm thinking of selling it." He was talking about the Jag.

I stood beside him and looked at the shapely old car. It was black and had a soft top, the kind that pulls back like a hood on a baby's pram. The paintwork was scratched and dented in places, but it still looked stately.

"I might get a few bob for it," he said.

I didn't answer.

He had bought the car in the summer as a kind of homage to his dad, who had died three years before in a car accident. His dad had always loved Jaguars but had never been able to afford one. Billy, who knew stacks about cars, had picked it up at an auction and decided to renovate it for his own use. That was before he'd spent a couple of weeks in Her Majesty's prison. I stood watching as a single ribbon of smoke curled up into the air.

"It's taking up space," he said.

I still didn't answer. I knew what he wanted me to say. He wanted me to try and talk him out of it, to be the sensible adult and tell him to pull himself together. I was fed up with it, though. Anyway, Billy and I were always *talking*; we spent our days saying sensible things to each other, giving advice, confiding dreams and ambitions. At other times we used talk as a kind of entertainment; gossiping, discussing films, politics, making fun of the world in general. No, in all the years I had known Billy we'd had our fair share of verbal communication.

Since Sunday night, in the car, when the rain had sounded like tiny footsteps on the roof, since then, I had tired of trying to talk things through. In among all the thoughts and irritations of the case there was this *longing* feeling that was swirling around inside my chest. I did not want to go back to square one with Billy and pretend that the kiss hadn't happened. I had done it too often.

"It's not as if I've really got the time or money to do the work on it," Billy said, still looking at the car, his cigarette sitting at the end of his fingers, the ash growing grey and flaky at the top.

I swallowed my nervousness and stepped across him, so that we were face to face.

"What's the matter, Patsy?" he said, in a low voice.

I didn't answer, I was fed up with explanations. I just kissed him. I had to stretch up to do it, but I put my hands on either side of his face and pulled him as close as I could, before I closed my eyes and rubbed my lips against his.

"Just a minute," he said and drew back. My heart dropped down to my knees as I opened my eyes, wondering why he had stopped. He dropped the cigarette on to the ground and looked at his own bare feet with annoyance.

"Allow me," I said, and squashed it into the floor as he took me by the shoulders and pulled me back towards him.

Lisa Black opened the front door of her house and took me up two flights of stairs to a tiny flat. She was wearing a light-coloured sweatshirt with a hood over some jogging trousers. On her feet she had bright red, thick socks with rubberized soles. Her hair was dark blonde, much darker at the roots.

I'd been worried that she wouldn't speak to me, but she talked non-stop from the moment I stepped into the house. I barely had time to take notes.

"I've already spoken to the police about it. When I heard about Louise's accident I couldn't believe it. But was it an accident? That's what I've been asking myself over and over. She was worried about that young man, spent the whole time she was here looking out the window, afraid that he would come. I kept saying, Louise, how can anyone know you're here? I only moved into the flat two weeks ago! Two weeks last Friday to be exact. Would you like a cup of tea?"

I shook my head and took a seat in a tiny cold kitchenette. Even though it was mild outside, there was a chill in the room. I noticed that Lisa Black was wearing a jumper underneath her sweatshirt.

From time to time she pulled the hood tightly round her neck as though it was a scarf. I was about to ask her a couple of questions when she started speaking again.

"Louise got here about lunchtime, I think. She sat in that very chair that you're sitting in now and she told me that she'd been staying at Sherry's. That didn't surprise me, she and Sherry were always close."

"Straight from Sherry's." I made a note and heard Lisa Black start again.

"It was Sherry and me who started at Jingles first. The very same week actually. We were good pals, we got on well together. Then Louise came. She and Sherry just clicked! Everyone was surprised at how quickly they became close. I wasn't and I didn't mind it one little bit. Some of the other dancers thought my feelings were hurt, but I said to them, it's up to Sherry who she's friends with! She's not my property. No, I didn't mind, not one little bit."

She gave a smile and began to rub her hands together rapidly as though she was feeling the cold. I noticed her nails then, blood red, carefully manicured.

"I kept friendly with both of them. They did a lot of stuff together, though; shopping, double dates, cinema, things like that. I couldn't always make it."

"Did anyone come to see her?"

Lisa Black shook her head adamantly, as if I'd just suggested something illegal.

"No. She stayed here a couple of hours. Made a couple of phone calls on her mobile. She loved that mobile. I said to Sherry, Louise is certainly attached to her mobile!"

"I don't suppose you know who she rang?"

"No. I left her on her own. Until she got into a state. Then I stayed with her. She was always a bit of a cry baby. Highly strung, Sherry said she was."

"Jack Ross? She was crying about him? That's understandable," I said. "I was there, only metres away from where he was killed."

"Oh no, I shouldn't think she was crying about Jack Ross. Not Jack Ross at all. I said to some of the other dancers, she won't stick with Jack Ross, not at all. Louise got bored easily."

"I thought she and Jack Ross were getting engaged?"

"So did he. But I think Louise was just stringing him along. I said to Sherry, Louise just strings people along. Not that I minded. It didn't have anything to do with me, after all. If she wanted to two-time her bloke it was up to her."

She leant back in her chair, opened a drawer and pulled out an emery-board.

"Two-time him?" I said, scribbling. I was having trouble keeping up with her.

"No one at the dance studio believed me when I told them. It was only about three weeks ago, I think. I saw her in a car with someone. I didn't think anything of it, you know. I didn't see who he was, but when she got out she came straight over to me and said, *You didn't see me, Lisa. Please don't tell a soul. It would upset Jack and his parents. Promise you won't say anything, especially not to Sherry.* She was almost hysterical. She confided in me. *I'm in love with him, Lisa*, she said. *He's so different to Jack.* I was surprised that she told me and not Sherry. What with them being so close." She started to shape one of her nails, holding it up to the light and then sawing gently at it with the emery-board.

"Louise was with someone else?" I sat for a minute trying to take it in.

"Sherry wouldn't hear a word against Louise, but I said to her, I said, Sherry, Louise has got an under-handed way about her. Sherry was too loyal for her own good, though."

"Sherry Stevens didn't say anything about it," I said.

"She's not the sort to gossip. Not Sherry."

"Did anyone else know about this other relation-ship?" I said.

"No. That was the funny thing. If I hadn't seen her getting out of his car nobody would have known! Sherry was quite upset at the gossip, because she liked Jack Ross. She got quite angry with me. It didn't bother me, though. It didn't bother me one little bit. There!"

She held a perfect red nail in the air for me to see.

I left Lisa in her cold kitchenette and walked out into the street feeling exhausted, my ears still vibrating from her stream of chatter. I'd got most of it down in my notes. Louise had had someone else. It was something I hadn't considered. It didn't fit in at all. She and Jack were supposed to be the perfect couple. I kept remembering Mrs Palmer's wish for them to have a nice detached house in Essex.

It changed things. There was no doubt about that. I packed my notepad into my bag and made my way to work.

I was about an hour late and I wondered if Tony would be annoyed. I kept rehearsing names of shops and photocopiers to keep up my story. I was surprised, though, when I walked through the office door and found Tony sitting in my chair, at my desk. In front of him was a packet of Hobnobs that had been opened. He was just dipping one into a cup of something when I arrived. He jumped up.

"Patricia!" He said it guiltily. I assumed it was to do with the Hobnobs.

"Yes, I'm sorry, it took longer than I thought it would." I put my jacket on the hook and walked across to the kettle. I saw, on the side, a cup set out for me, a tea bag inside.

"Kettle's only just boiled," Tony said, standing behind me. "Do you want me to do it for you?"

"No, I'll manage," I said.

Something was wrong. I let the hot water pour on to the tea bag and wondered what it was. A feeling of apprehension was cautiously tiptoeing into my stomach. My uncle Tony never offered to do anything for me. He obviously had some bad news.

"Patricia, I..."

"What's wrong?" I said, turning to face him.

The first thing that came into my head was that something was up with my mum. She was ill and hadn't told me. The back of my neck plaited up in readiness for bad news.

"Patricia, you know that business is awful..."

I felt all my muscles relax as he spoke. It was nothing important. It was only to do with the business.

"...and the trouble is that the agency simply cannot go on as it is."

"Yes, I thought that," I said. Maybe it was a good time to tell him about the new letters I had written.

"The nature of this work is, well, like the tide, it comes and it goes..."

The tide. I had a picture of the sea in my head and watched as he took another biscuit from the packet. I wanted to ask him what had happened to his diet.

"And we simply can't sustain two salaries as well

as the computer."

"The computer is essential," I said, looking at it sitting on the desk, creamy and solid.

"So I'm going to have to let you go." He sat back, his eyes avoiding mine.

"Let me go where?" I said, puzzled.

"Let you go," he repeated, and when I didn't say anything he added, "to another job."

"You mean you're sacking me?" I said, the penny finally dropping like a cannonball behind me.

"I wouldn't say *sacking*, I wouldn't use that term, just temporarily, for the present, suggesting that you..."

"You're firing me!" I said in astonishment.

"...try and find a job somewhere else, for the foreseeable future."

"But I put off going to university!" I said.

"That was your choice, Patricia. There was never any pressure from me." He stood up, flustered. "You must be sensible about this," he said, picking up the packet of biscuits and tipping them into a biscuit tin on the side. A biscuit tin that I had chosen and bought. Just like the computer that I had suggested and helped to shop for. Now I was being sacked.

"How can you do this?" I whined.

"It's not personal. You must know that I'd rather do anything than let you go. I owe it to your mother, but I have no choice. I'll pay you for another couple of weeks, but I don't expect you to work. You can use the office for phoning round, looking for new jobs, typing a CV."

"Thanks very much!" I said, picking up my rucksack and grabbing my jacket from the hook.

"I'll help you look for another job," he said.

I looked at him standing beside *my* desk, his fingers drumming on *my* computer monitor, his biscuits inside *my* biscuit tin. I thought of his daughter, Sarah, who worked in an insurance company and wondered what he would say if they gave her the sack.

"You'll see. A bright girl like you – we'll find you a new job in no time."

I was fit to explode and tell him what I thought of him, his vanity and his silly diet and his detective skills that belonged to a bygone era. But what was the point?

"I think I'll go home," I said steadily.

"You do that," Tony said, his forehead all creased up, as though I was ill. He opened the office door for me and for one horrible moment I thought he was going to hug me.

"Oh," he said, "I nearly forgot, this came for you." He reached into the mail tray and gave me a large brown envelope. On the outside, above the address, were the words PATSY KELLY URGENT. I took it, shoved it into my rucksack and left without a word. As I was going down the stairs, out to the street, I could hear Tony's voice saying, *You'll see, it'll be all right. We'll find you a new job in no time.*

Who was he kidding? Hadn't he heard about unemployment among the young? I gave the door at the bottom of the stairs an angry slam and then went out into the street.

I sat on a bench near the big shopping mall and felt nonplussed. Sacked! In the middle of a case! I looked around and saw young women of my own age walking purposefully, as though they had somewhere to go; a shop that they sold clothes in, an office phone that was waiting to be answered, a computer that said *Good morning* when they switched it on.

It wasn't fair. It wasn't right.

I saw the corner of the envelope sticking out of my rucksack and pulled it out. It was A4 size and on the back there was a scribbled note. *Here's the enlargements. Let me know if you see anything. DM.* DM, Doctor Martin – no, Des Murray.

Even though I didn't feel like it, I pulled the photos out. I had no job, no university place to go to, but I still had the case to work on. I pursed my lips and pulled out the dozen or so A4 size photographs from the envelope. A quick flick through them showed groups of blurred faces. I took a slower look, ignoring the toing and froing of the shoppers around me. I saw myself in three of them. My red felt hat, my profile, most of my face in another. The images were blurred from having been blown up and expressions and facial features weren't always that clear. I worked through them quietly, looking for any sign of Kevin Cooke's baby features.

He wasn't there. I looked carefully at dozens of faces, but there was no one who remotely resembled him. I felt a door shut lightly in my face and slumped back on to the bench.

I was going to have to stop hitting my head against a brick wall. I simply couldn't prove that Kevin Cooke was on the platform and that was that.

There had to be some other way to find Louise's killer.

# 16

# The Meeting

I rang Billy on the mobile and asked him to come and pick me up. I couldn't even raise a smile when he said, "Anything for you, madam," in a half-sarcastic way.

There was nothing else for it. I would have to tell Des Murray that there was nothing on the enlargements. I pictured his sneering expression and his *I told you so* tone of voice.

A dark grey cloud the size of Asia seemed to descend to within metres of the rooftops around me. Then it rained. It was all I needed. My glasses became splattered and I took them off and pushed them, along with the photos, into my rucksack and edged under the canopy of a nearby shop to shelter.

After about ten minutes, I heard the sound of a

car horn and I saw Billy pull up on the opposite side of the road. I zigzagged between the slow moving traffic and got into the car. Billy gave me a tiny smile. Perry was there as well.

"I'm just giving Perry a lift down the London Hospital. Why aren't you at work?" Billy said. "I thought you were only working on the case in your spare time?"

"My uncle sacked me, made me redundant, whatever. On top of that I've hit a dead end," I said, grumpily.

"Oh Patsy, you've been sacked!" Billy said.

"That's three of us without a job!" Perry said, cheerfully.

Billy pursed his lips and looked as though he didn't know what to say. Neither did I. I sat quietly as we drove towards central London, its skyscrapers in the distance, full up with busy *working* people, who got wages in their bank accounts every month. I ran my finger over the envelope of enlargements that was sticking out of my bag and thought that what I really should do was to go straight to the police station and face Des Murray.

"You know why they call it the 'sack', Patsy?" Perry said, as we were creeping along in a traffic jam.

"No, but I bet you're going to tell me," I said, as pleasantly as I could. Up in front of us I could see the buildings of the London Hospital.

"Because, in the olden days, when the boss didn't want you any more, he gave you a sack to put all your stuff in. An actual sack, see?"

"An *actual* sack," I said, smiling in spite of my bad mood.

"Not a *virtual* sack?" Billy said, joining in.

"No, straight up. A brown sack that you put your stuff in."

Me and Billy couldn't help but smile at each other. Perry just sat looking pleased with himself. We were like a family, the parents in the front and the kid in the back seat.

A family. It was such an important unit. Everywhere you looked there was stuff about Family Values, the Importance of the Family, Family Loyalty. And yet, in the cases I'd investigated, often family had played a part somewhere in the violent death of someone.

"Come in and see Joey Hooper," Perry said. "He could probably do with the company."

I looked at Billy and he nodded in an easygoing way. Why not? I thought. It wasn't as if I had anything *pressing* to do. We found a parking meter and walked the short distance to the hospital, Perry jauntily out in front of us.

"You know what?" I said to Billy as the three of us stood waiting for the lift. "The bones of the Elephant Man are kept here, and not only that," I smiled at Perry, "Michael Jackson offered millions to buy them."

"Well, fancy that!" Billy said as the doors to the lift glided open.

Joey Hooper was sitting by his brother's bed with a book. His lips were moving and I guessed that he was reading aloud.

"He's in a different position," I said. Paul Hooper was on his side, his back towards me. "Has he moved?" I said to Perry.

"No. The nurses are always moving him about. It's to stop bed sores forming," Perry said knowledgeably.

"Oh."

A few moments later Joey glanced sideways through the window at us and gestured. We waited while he read for a further few minutes and then he came out. He was rubbing his head where the "H" was sculpted into his hair.

"All right, Patsy, Perry? Who's this?"

"This is Billy Rogers," I said. Billy gave Joey a nod.

"How's Paul?" I said, looking in at the boy in the bed.

"So-so. About the same."

"I saw a film about some people who come out of comas," Perry said, looking thoughtful. "'Awakenings' it was called, or something like that. It was true, like, based on real life. Straight up."

"OK, Perry. I'm off home now to see me mum. You tell me about it along the way."

"We could give you a lift," Billy said.

"Good man," Joey said and gave Billy a friendly pat on the back.

I watched the three of them walk ahead down the hospital corridors, talking easily. Now and then Joey Hooper lifted his hand to pat Perry's shoulder. They looked like three friends on their way out for the evening. A wave of sadness hit me for the boy in the bed who in all probability would never go out for the evening again.

In the lift, on the way down, Joey Hooper suddenly said, "The Elephant Man's bones are kept here, did you know that? Michael Jackson wanted to pay millions for them. That's a tonne of money, you know what I'm saying?"

I began to giggle. I couldn't help it. The three of them looked curiously at me as the laughter spurted out.

Joey Hooper chatted all the way home. His dad managed a pub at Finsbury Park. His mum worked as a receptionist in a doctor's. His brother Paul had been a passionate supporter of the Arsenal. He'd gone to every game, home or away, since he'd been about thirteen. When they'd moved to Highbury, Paul Hooper thought he had died and gone to heaven.

It was an unfortunate choice of words, I thought.

Perry kept interrupting Joey, adding bits of information. *Paul Hooper played brilliant football. He was in the school's first team even though he was too young. All the other kids were really jealous of him. And the weights, don't forget about the weight training.*

When we parked at Highbury, Joey Hooper said, "My brother was full of life and the Cookes knocked it out of him. And what did the police do? Nothing."

None of us answered. Years ago, Billy would have remonstrated with him, told him to sue somebody. Now he just sat silently. I watched as Joey Hooper wriggled about on the seat, his hand in his jeans pocket. He pulled out a newspaper cutting from a daily paper, Monday's edition. A single column with a photo of Louise Palmer at the top. The headline was GIRLFRIEND OF STABBED BOY DIES IN MYSTERIOUS CIRCUMSTANCES. It was a glamorous shot of Louise and I wondered whether her mother had sorted it out for them.

"I saw this in the paper yesterday. It reminded me of something. Remember I told you that I used to shadow Lee Cooke before he'd been put away?"

"Yes?" I said.

"A couple of times, in that week leading up to Bonfire Night, I shadowed Lee. Nothing unusual, I was just passing time, after I'd seen Paul."

None of us answered. I found myself looking at

Louise Palmer's brilliant smile in the photograph. Lisa Black's words came into my head: *Louise was just stringing him along.*

"I see him meet this girl, in McDonald's it was. Twice. She's really good-looking, walks straight up to him each time. No smile, no nothing. They sit down in one of the tables and talk, five, maybe ten minutes. Then Lee gets up to go. I don't know her from Adam, not till I see her face in the newspaper."

"Louise Palmer met Lee Cooke twice?" I said. "You mean like a *romantic* meeting?"

"It didn't look like that to me. There was no friendliness there and it was only for ten minutes, no more. Then Lee looked hacked off and moved on. Both times, he went straight round to the Panther Gym, where his brother hangs out. I'm telling you it didn't look like no romance to me."

"Why would she have met Lee Cooke?" Billy said.

"Don't ask me. All I know is that a few days later her boyfriend is stabbed by this same Lee Cooke. Know what I'm saying?"

I did know what he was saying and I thought it was very funny indeed.

After Joey Hooper got out of the car, we sat there for a few minutes. The rain had cleared and some fingers of sunlight were poking through the clouds. A sweet shop across the road still had a sign in it that said FIREWORKS FOR SALE. It was almost two weeks since Jack Ross had been stabbed, less than three days since Louise Palmer had gone under the train, and everything was starting to look different. Jack Ross and the Cooke brothers weren't the enemies that I'd thought they were, and Louise Palmer had had a dark side to her life.

I felt Billy's hand on the back of my neck and gave him a little smile.

"Sorry about the job," he said.

I nodded but I was still thinking about Louise. Why had she met with Lee Cooke? And then only days later her boyfriend was stabbed. It was odd.

"I need to speak to Kevin Cooke," I said, grabbing Billy's hand and giving it a squeeze.

"That's not wise," Billy said.

"You don't want to do that, Patsy," Perry said, "you want to keep right out of his way."

"But if I just knew what the meeting between Lee and Louise was about. I've got to talk to him. The case isn't going anywhere, if anything it's getting more complicated. You know him, Perry. Can't you set me up with a meeting?"

"I don't hang round with him. You know that."

"Even if Perry could arrange for you to speak to Kevin Cooke, why should he want to speak to you? What's in it for him?" Billy said, earnestly.

I couldn't answer him. It was true. There was no reason on earth why Kevin Cooke should speak to me. I tapped my fingers on the envelope in my bag. If only there had been a photo of him on the platform. Then he'd have to speak to me.

"I know," I said, suddenly. "Perry, you go and see Kevin Cooke and tell him I've got a photograph of him that places him on the platform at Oxford Circus on the night Louise died."

"But you haven't," Billy said, puzzled.

"I know that but Kevin Cooke doesn't. It'll give me an excuse to speak to him. The fact that I haven't got a photo won't matter to him, it'll be something that he'll be pleased about."

"I don't like it," Perry said quietly.

"Neither do I," Billy added.

"Me neither. But it's got to be done and that's that!" I said crossly.

# 17
# Kevin Cooke

It took Perry a while to get to speak to Kevin Cooke. Eventually he rang me and said that Cooke would see me on Thursday lunchtime at the Panther Gym at Stratford Broadway. Billy had wanted to go with me but Perry had advised against it. Kevin Cooke wouldn't feel threatened by a woman, he'd said, but if a bloke came it would only create macho tension. He hadn't used those exact words but I'd known what he meant.

Most of Wednesday I'd hung around at home. I'd not yet told my mum that I'd been sacked and I supposed that my uncle had not had the courage to tell her either. I got a local paper and scanned it unsuccessfully for jobs. My mum was busy with college work and I guessed from the amount of perfume she'd put on that she was seeing her boyfriend Gerry during the day. I let her out of the house and watched her walk down the pathway to her car. She had a fitted suit on and her hair was hanging thickly over her shoulders. She was much too good for the overweight and opinionated Gerry.

I was reminded of the time, not so long before, when I had caught Gerry in the arms of another woman. I had been furious and full of moral indignation. Then Brian Martin came into my head. How long had he stood watching while me and Billy were kissing in the car? I shook my head at the embarrassment of it.

I thought of Louise Palmer. Her secret side had unbalanced the whole case. At first it had been simple. Kevin Cooke was trying to get her out of the way so that she wouldn't testify against his brother. But now even that first murder was not so clean cut. Jack Ross had been friendly with the Cookes. Jack Ross's girlfriend had met with his killer only days before his death.

Jack Ross's *girlfriend*. Was she really that? One of her closest friends had seen her in a car with another man. She had admitted it, said that the man was *so different to Jack*. Who was he? Did it have any relevance to the case?

On Thursday morning I got dressed up. I spent ages on my hair and put reasonably heavy make-up on, dark eye shadow and plum lipstick. I found a dress that I hadn't worn for some time and put it on with a loose lacy shirt over the top. Then my leather jacket. I decided against a hat but took a long pink chiffon scarf with me. I wasn't trying to impress anybody, I was covering up my nervousness, using my clothes and make-up as a kind of armour.

Just as I was leaving the house the phone rang. I let the answer-phone pick it up. It was Des Murray. His voice was gravelly and there wasn't a hint of a smile anywhere. Had I found anything in the photos? Could I go down to the station? There'd been a development.

I shook my head sadly, then nodded as if I was actually speaking to him. Maybe I also would have a development to report to him. I walked out of the house for the first time in two days and felt the air, crisp and sharp. The sky was the lightest blue, not a cloud in sight. I hunched my shoulders with the chill and wished I'd put a jumper on instead of a blouse.

I felt like I was meeting royalty. I got to the gym about one o'clock and sat in the foyer fidgeting around as though I was there for a job interview. Just for something to do I got my notepad out of my bag. Kevin Cooke walked in at that moment and gave it and me a frown.

"No notes," he said sternly, "just a chat, Perry said."

I nodded and wondered what had happened to my voice. If I didn't pull myself together soon I wouldn't get anything out of the meeting at all. I tried to remind myself that it probably wasn't that long since Kevin Cooke had been careering round the streets on his BMX stunt bike.

In my rucksack, there was a sealed envelope with one of the enlargements in it. I'd picked the most blurred one that I could find and drawn a red felt ring around the face of a young white man. It could have been anyone. Underneath I wrote, *Kevin Cooke.* I'd also circled the date and the time.

He sat opposite me, in a black leather chair. There was no one else around, just the sounds of distant footsteps from the floor above. The street door was closed behind me and the windows frosted over, so that I couldn't see out and nobody could see in. I had to admit it, I felt uneasy.

"I haven't got much time, Patsy. Perry says you've got something to show me. Why don't we have a look at it?"

He sat down in the chair opposite me, his legs hanging apart, his hands loosely joined together. There was a faint smile somewhere around his eyes. I wondered if he was remembering the morning that he had followed me.

"I wanted to talk to you about your brother," I started.

"Come on, Patsy. Let's see the photo." He snapped

his fingers twice, as if I were a dog that had to be brought to heel. I pulled myself together, coughed and zipped up the top of my rucksack.

"Last Saturday night, I was supposed to meet Louise Palmer on the Central Line platform at Oxford Circus station. I know for a fact that you were there when she was killed." I said it as aggressively as I could.

"You saw me there?" Kevin Cooke exhaled. "Actually there on the platform?"

"Yes, and I have a photograph to prove it," I lied.

"So how come I'm not under arrest now?"

"Because I haven't shown it to the police yet. It's not absolutely conclusive. I need to ask you some more things about the case before I can be sure."

"But you've brought it with you?" he said and snapped his fingers again at me. I held tightly on to my bag.

"Let's see it, Patsy."

I was about to shake my head firmly when he leant forward, gave me a shove sideways and made a grab for my rucksack. I had a job not falling off the chair and my arm smarted. He pulled out the envelope and dumped the bag on the floor in the middle of us. Some of my stuff spilled out, my purse, my comb, my notebooks, my scarf. I rubbed my arm and steadied myself, breathing in shallowly. The sight of my things on the floor made me feel weak.

Kevin Cooke looked at the photograph for a few seconds and then smiled. "This is a joke. You've been having a little joke with me."

"You were there, on that platform," I said stubbornly.

"Who told you that? Joey Hooper? The fact is, it doesn't matter either way because I was nowhere near Lou Palmer when she went under the train. This photo is worthless and you know it."

He took a corner of the photo in each hand and pulled it apart so that it tore in two. Then he doubled them up and did the same again. The pieces of the photo floated down on top of my up-ended rucksack. I wanted to leave. If I'd had the courage, I probably would have got up and walked out. I sat there, though, while he shook his head and his mouth relaxed into a smile, as though he was sharing a joke with himself. I wondered how he could take things so lightly. Jack Ross dead, his own brother in prison, Louise Palmer dead. His name, his face, popping up everywhere. A tiny idea came into my head.

"I'm surprised that you're so calm," I said, "for someone who is about to be picked up on conspiracy charges."

"Do what?"

"I know the evidence about you pushing Louise Palmer off the platform is weak. Maybe you didn't do it, I'm not saying you did. There's another interpretation for all this, though."

Kevin Cooke raised his eyebrows pleasantly.

"I've been told that you, your brother and Jack Ross beat up Paul Hooper."

Kevin Cooke shook his head. "Not true."

"Two weeks ago Jack Ross was killed by Lee. This is after he's been seen meeting with Jack's girlfriend and then coming to see you."

"So?" Kevin Cooke said, his eyebrows raised.

"Let's say that Jack Ross was feeling guilty, had decided to make a clean breast of it to the police. Louise, his girlfriend, comes and tells Lee and Lee comes to you and together you decide that he's got to be taught a lesson."

I was making it up as I went along. It was like the plot of an American TV show. I was picturing Louise as a *femme fatale* from an old film, trapped in a relationship that only murder could get her out of. The strange thing was that Kevin Cooke wasn't laughing any more. I sensed that I was getting warm.

"Lee takes it too far, killing Jack. He's in prison and Louise Palmer is the only one who knows about it. Then she dies and we know that you were at Oxford Circus on that night. Maybe you didn't push her, maybe she just saw you and got the fright of her life and then fell on to the line. There's still enough to get you on conspiracy, though, and you could still go to prison for that."

"This is rubbish," Kevin Cooke said, but I noticed that he had started playing with the knuckles of one hand, as if he were about to crack them one by one. "What's the girlfriend got to do with anything? Why should she tell Lee what Jack was going to do?"

"She had her reasons. I know that she'd been seeing some other bloke. Maybe she was fed up with Jack and wanted him out of the way."

"So just pack him in then."

"She saw Lee, then Lee came to you, then Jack was dead. That's conspiracy, Kevin, whether you like it or not. It won't worry her now, but it could be a problem for you."

"You got this all wrong," Kevin Cooke said quietly. "Let me give you some suggestions that you can chew over. Nothing comes back to me, understand that, nothing. I am clean."

I held my breath and looked at Kevin Cooke. Something in what I had said had worried him. I waited for him to speak.

"You say that Jack Ross was one of three people who beat up Paul Hooper. You're wrong about that."

"He was seen."

"Yes, someone was seen but it wasn't Jack."

I was about to disagree again, to argue my point. Then some cogs started working in my head.

"You mean that it wasn't Jack who did the beating, but his brother, Frank? Frank Ross beat up Paul Hooper?"

"And enjoyed it too, as I remember."

"But Frank Ross works in a solicitor's!" I said with astonishment.

"Louise Palmer did come to Lee a couple of weeks ago and said that Jack was fed up with being put in the frame for Paul Hooper's condition. She said that he had plans to go to the police and tell what he knew. She said she didn't like the idea of him grassing up his mates and wanted Lee to warn him, to frighten him a little."

"She really did tell Lee that?" I said, hardly believing my ears. My own made-up story was coming true.

"Lee came to see me. We talked it over and decided that we would have a talk with him. Trouble is that Lee couldn't wait. Lee went too far and Jack ended up dead. Then, instead of keeping quiet about it, Louise Palmer tells the police it was Lee. She tells them!"

"So you threatened her?"

"I just jogged her memory. If Lee got done for the stabbing, then the truth would come out that she'd set Jack up for it."

"So she ran away."

"I got the word on Saturday that Louise was giving herself up to the police. I went down to Oxford Circus to see her, to make sure that she knew what the score was, but I didn't get there in time."

"She'd already fallen on to the tracks."

"There were people being brought off, some hysterical types. When I saw something had happened, I just stood back behind a group of people and watched."

"So you really weren't there?"

"I've never said I wasn't at the station. How could I? The Law came between me and Joey Hooper in the ticket office. They took my name. I can't deny it. But I wasn't on the platform when she went under."

I must have had disappointment written all over my face, because Kevin Cooke leant forward and said, "If you want to know what was going on on the platform why don't you ask your pal Joey Hooper? He was there. I saw him walking past at the speed of light."

"Joey Hooper wasn't on the platform!" I said.

"Is that what he told you, Patsy?"

"He was arguing with you, afterwards in the ticket office."

"Didn't you think that was a bit funny, though, Patsy?" Kevin Cooke said. "Starting an argument in the middle of a public place. Could Joey have been setting up an alibi for himself? Who knows? Ask him. He's your friend."

"I have to go," I said. I needed to think.

"Just remember one thing. None of this comes back to me. No more photos, no more threats. I'm not part of this." Kevin Cooke stood up.

“What about Lee?” I said, kneeling down to pick up my stuff.

“Lee’ll have to look after himself,” he said, holding the door of the gym open. Outside, I could see the traffic streaming past. I hauled my rucksack over my shoulder and walked past him.

So much for brotherly love, I thought.

# 18

# The Late Witness

It was three o'clock when Billy dropped me off at the police station. While I was waiting for Des Murray to come and sign me in, Heather Warren walked through. She smiled when she saw me. She was wearing what looked like a man's suit, dark brown with pinstripes. Around her neck was a bright orange scarf. In her hand she had what looked like a giant filofax.

"Patsy. I'm glad I've caught you. How are you getting on with Des?"

"Fine," I said. I noticed that the desk sergeant had stood upright and put aside the newspaper that he'd been reading.

"I talked to that friend of mine over at Highbury. You remember I told you I would. About the Hooper boy?"

"Yes?" I said hopefully.

"Not much joy, I'm afraid. He said that it was thoroughly investigated. There was simply no evidence that the Cooke brothers attacked Paul Hooper. The boy himself, being in a coma, is not a witness and there was no one else around."

I shook my head disconsolately.

"What about Louise Palmer? Des told me you looked at the station video?"

Just then the inside door opened and Des Murray came out. He had his mouth open to say something but stopped when he saw Heather. He nodded curtly at her and held the door open for me to go in.

"It's all a bit blurred," I said.

I walked to the door and she smiled at me. "That's the thing with videos. Get Des to have some enlargements done."

"Right," I said and followed Des. We walked along a corridor and up a flight of stairs in complete silence. In the CID room I sat down at Des's desk. He looked grumpy as usual, pulled a roll out of a paper bag and bit into it.

"Late lunch," he mumbled.

"Don't mind me," I said, knowing full well that he wouldn't. He chewed hard and his eyes seemed to bounce round the room. I took the enlargements out of my bag and plonked them on the table between us.

"I can't find anything of significance in these," I

said, while he was still chewing. "And I've been asking round, through contacts that I have, and I can't actually place Cooke on the platform when I was meeting Louise."

A tiny smile appeared on his face. It was the closest I'd seen to him being happy. I ignored it and went on to tell him about Frank Ross's involvement in the Paul Hooper case and Louise's meeting with Lee Cooke and the fact that she had a mystery boyfriend.

"Not that we know whether these things are relevant to this case or not," he said when I'd finished.

"No," I said, closing my mouth. I'd done my bit, I'd informed them of what I'd found out. Except for Kevin Cooke's suggestion that Joey Hooper had been on the platform when Louise was killed. I hadn't yet decided what to do with that particular bit of the puzzle.

"You said you had a development to tell me about," I said, after a few moments.

Without looking at me he opened a file and tossed a sheet of closely written paper across. "Late witness," he said.

I looked at the statement in front of me. It was signed by someone called Ben Fryer. It was in neat, slanted handwriting:

*I was on the platform on Saturday waiting for a train so that I could go to Tottenham Court Road. I have a music pitch there. I play a guitar and I earn a fair bit, especially on a Saturday night. I didn't have a ticket so I was keeping out of the way of Inspectors. I saw the girl, just seconds before she went off the platform. Everyone was looking up at some kid's balloon, but I had my eye open in case there was any Transport Police around. She seemed to be pushing her way through the crowd. It all happened very quickly and what I saw was over in a flash. A kid came out of nowhere and pushed her. He was wearing a grey hooded sweatshirt that looked really big. I didn't see his face. I just see him give her a shove and then I walked forward. I suppose in the back of my head I thought I could of pulled her back. No sooner I took a step than the train came past and I don't remember much for the next few minutes. I was shocked. Like I felt paralysed for a few minutes. Then all the screaming started and I saw these Underground Inspectors coming on the platform. I just legged it. I had no ticket, see. If I'd come forward I would've got into trouble. I thought loads of people would've seen it so I didn't think it would matter if I just got out of the way. Ben Fryer.*

"Why come forward now?" I said.

"Guilty conscience? Who knows?"

"A grey hooded sweatshirt," I said, trying to picture the scene.

"Great clue, isn't it? You know how many shops supply those tops? You know how common it is? You could walk from here down to the end of the road and see half a dozen people wearing one. We'll have to look through dozens of videotapes now."

"Why? I thought we'd already looked through them."

"The murderer was wearing a grey hooded top. He must have escaped during the panic. There are a dozen video cameras at Oxford Circus station. One of them may have picked him up. I need you here, tomorrow morning, to help look through them."

It wasn't a request. It was an order.

"I'm supposed to be going to Louise Palmer's funeral," I said, "or will it be held up now? Now that we know she was pushed?"

"Nope. You think about it. There's not a lot that we can learn from Louise's body. At least what's left of it."

"No, I suppose not," I said, refusing to let myself picture Louise Palmer's remains.

"Nope. I think it might be a good thing for them to go ahead with the funeral. I might wander along myself. It's a fact, you know, Patsy, that murderers often go to the funeral of their victims. Arsonists like to hang round and watch the fire they started, so a killer likes to see the wooden box and the flowers."

There was another smile on Des Murray's lips. He was looking forward to it.

I went out through the security doors at the back of

the station and I pulled my jacket tightly round me as I walked through the car park. Looking for the exit, my eye settled on a blue Metro that was parking against the wall in the space marked for visitors.

Brian Martin got out of it and I stopped for a second. I did not want to see him. Embarrassment rose up around my throat. He was locking his driver's door and hadn't seen me. I looked frantically around for an exit where I could slip away without having to come face to face with him, but there was none. I guessed that he had come to the station to see his dad, who was a uniformed officer. I had no choice, I would have to speak to him. My shoulders hunched, a humble expression on my face, I walked towards him.

He caught sight of me and I opened my mouth to speak, but he gave me a withering look and then turned away. I took a couple of steps after him, but he quickened his pace and within minutes had opened and closed the heavy glass wing doors to the police station and left me standing there.

He hated me.

I shook my head and turned to go, but had to wait for a few seconds as a police car screeched into the car park and pulled up a few metres away from me. A policeman and woman got out. Between them was a young black boy who was protesting his innocence loudly. He was handcuffed at the front and kept raising both his hands together while he was speaking. He had a grey hooded sweatshirt top on, the type that the witness said Louise's killer had been wearing. Des Murray was right. They were very common. I remembered Billy had had one some months before. The policeman took the young black man's arm and led him towards the doors, and I was reminded of the night of Louise's murder when I was in the ticket office and I saw Joey Hooper arguing with Kevin Cooke. There'd been a policeman then, I recalled, trying to calm the argument down, leading Joey Hooper away. Kevin Cooke had said that Joey set up the argument so as to create an alibi for himself. Could that have been true?

Then I remembered an important fact. Joey Hooper had been wearing a grey hooded sweatshirt and jogging pants. The hood had been down, laying on his shoulders, his head bare, the "H" standing out, obvious to everyone that was passing.

*A grey hooded sweatshirt.*

It gave me a bad feeling. I liked Joey Hooper. I felt outraged about what had happened to his brother. Why would he want to murder Louise Palmer? It didn't make sense.

# 19
# Dead

The London Hospital was extraordinarily busy. Nurses seemed to be rushing here and there with trolleys and trays; doctors, their white coats flapping, were writing on clipboards and talking into wall phones. The woman on reception seemed to be dealing with three people at once, looking red-faced and harassed. To top it all a man was wandering aimlessly in circles holding a can of Special Brew, humming a tune, his free hand conducting an imaginary orchestra. I walked past quickly, but had to stand and wait for the lift. I pressed the lift button three or four times and began to tap my fingers against the wall. Both of the lifts seemed to be stuck up on the eighth floor and I thought about taking the stairs.

I turned away looking at the notices on the wall. The Asthma Society, Coping with Hepatitis, Living with Cystic Fibrosis, Prevention of Diabetes. Underneath were several small postcards. One of them caught my eye. "Wheelchair for sale, hardly ever used."

I just couldn't believe that Joey Hooper would have pushed Louise in front of a train. It was Jack Ross, Lee and Kevin Cooke that he blamed for his brother's death. Why would he have pushed Louise?

I looked at the light indicator which showed the lift still up at eight. I banged the button for the last time and decided to walk.

Eight flights of stairs later and I had no breath left. I stood at the top and let my lungs suck in air while my heart pounded like a drum against my rib-cage. I simply wasn't fit enough. Recovering and walking along the corridor to Nelson Ward I tried to work out what I was going to say to him. Should I tell him, for instance, that it was *Frank* Ross who had beaten his brother up? I didn't know.

I turned into the ward and was hit by the food smells that came from the giant aluminium trolley that was being pushed up the centre. I side-stepped it and walked on, but when I got to the side ward I stopped abruptly.

It was empty. Through the glass where Paul Hooper had lain there was just a bed, its sheets and covers made up tightly like a parcel. The door to the bedside cabinet was open and I could see that there was nothing inside it. On top of it was a vase with water, but no flowers.

"Can I help you?" a young nurse said.

"I've come to see Paul Hooper."

"Are you family?"

"No, I'm, I'm his brother's girlfriend," I lied.

"Oh, I'm terribly sorry. I think you should go home to Paul's family. They'll need you. I'm afraid Paul died last night."

"I don't understand, I just saw him the other day."

"A lung infection. Coma patients are prone to infections. He was given antibiotics, but it happened very fast. It was just after midnight. His family came up immediately."

I turned and looked at the empty bed. An orderly had gone into the room and was dusting and sweeping, opening the window to let the air in. They were getting it ready for a new patient.

Paul Hooper was really dead.

# 20
# Revenge

Louise Palmer's funeral was at ten o'clock. I wore a black hat and black scarf on top of my leather jacket. I took a small bunch of roses. I hadn't known Louise but I made the effort for her mother.

On top of her coffin was a dancer made completely out of white carnations. It reminded me of the figure you see on old-fashioned music boxes, the kind you wind up and then watch pirouette while some tinkly piano music plays.

The air in the cemetery was sharp and cold, the sky a piercing blue. Underfoot the grass seemed to crunch as it was stepped on and the wreaths looked chilly and exposed. The grave was halfway up a slope, the earth dug out of it and covered with fake grass. Mrs Palmer was dressed in black, her gold jewellery glinting in the bright sunlight, matching the brass handles of the sleek wood coffin. She was surrounded by the Ross family and several other people whom I didn't know. Sherry Stevens was there and hanging on to her arm was Lisa Black, her shoulders hunched up with the cold. There were about thirty school kids all in the dark uniform of Wood Road Comprehensive, my old school. Miss Eliot nodded across to me. I hadn't spoken to her since the beginning of the case. Perhaps I should have. She had been the one who had started it all off.

Frank Ross had a dark coloured suit on and kept his gaze down; on the ground, on the coffin, on the flowers. However hard I tried I couldn't seem to catch his eye. As the vicar spoke about death and grief being natural things I kept trying to imagine him and the Cookes beating up Paul Hooper. It just didn't sit right with his suit and his job in the solicitor's.

Paul Hooper. In a week or so there would be a funeral for him. On top of his coffin there might be a football made of carnations, in the Arsenal colours probably, red and white. The faces at that funeral would be mostly black. I looked around and saw that the faces in the cemetery then were exclusively white.

A hundred metres or so away I noticed Des Murray and another detective leaning against a tree.

He was lighting a cigarette, using his hands to cup the flame. I wondered if he had asked Frank Ross about his involvement with the Cookes. I knew I would find out later when I went to the station to look through the remainder of the videotapes.

I looked at the number of mourners that surrounded the grave. Louise was clearly popular. I had never known her but it seemed that she had been liked, loved even. People had spoken quite well of her; Miss Eliot, my old teacher, had thought she was worth making an effort for. So why had she gone to Lee Cooke and told him that Jack was going to go to the police? Surely she would have known that at the very least Jack would get a good hiding. OK, so she had someone new, but that didn't mean that she actually had to get her boyfriend *hurt*.

I sighed. Turning away from the mourners I looked at the group of wreaths that were banked up by the side of the grave. On the far left was one that must have been from Mr and Mrs Ross. *JACK AND LOUISE*, it said in dozens of small red roses.

Louise had stopped loving Jack Ross some time before, I knew that, so did Lisa Black and most of the people at the dance school. She had found someone new. Joey Hooper had said the meetings between Lisa and Lee Cooke hadn't looked like those of lovers. Could he have been wrong? It would have explained why she went to him and informed on her boyfriend. It would also have explained why

Lee Cooke ended up killing Jack Ross; an added motive of jealousy.

I took a couple of steps across to the flowers and looked at the tightly woven roses that must have cost a fortune. Beside it, in contrast, was the tiniest wreath of the lot; not a wreath at all more a bouquet, the kind a bride might carry. It was full of small, pastel-coloured blooms and fluffy foliage. Behind me I could hear the mourners mumbling and I was aware that the service had ended. I bent over to look at the flowers. *To Lou Lou, You and Jack together always. Frank.*

Lou Lou. It was a nickname I'd heard before. In fact, the whole phrase sounded familiar. I heard a number of car doors banging and looked to see people moving off down the incline. In the distance Des Murray was stubbing out his cigarette. *Lou Lou.* I'd heard Louise's name over and over in the last few days but that version of it I'd only seen once, or maybe twice. *You and Jack together always:* the words were familiar and yet different at the same time. I concentrated hard, closing my eyes to picture the words. They'd been written down, I remembered. *You and* me *together always*, that was it. That was the exact phrase that I remembered.

The love letters. Three carefully written letters on blue paper. Louise's keepsakes, the three of them, unsigned. I had thought they were from Jack.

I looked across the cemetery and saw Frank Ross

standing talking to Sherry Stevens and Lisa Black. Sherry Stevens was talking intently to him, one of her fingers in mid-air. A metre or so away Lisa Black was looking off into the distance, her shoulders humped as though she was miffed at something. Perhaps she felt left out again. I didn't know.

*Lou Lou, You and me together always.*

Frank Ross had been Louise's secret lover. Her boyfriend's brother. That was why she was so afraid of telling Jack. That was why she had gone to Lee Cooke. If Jack Ross had gone to the police it would have meant her new lover being arrested and Louise hadn't wanted that. Louise had fallen in love with her boyfriend's twin. Identical looks but more suave; wore suits and had a job in a solicitor's. Naturally she didn't want to tell Jack. Think of the upset it would have caused in the family. It made sense.

I started walking down the grassy slope after the mourners, in the direction of Frank Ross. Sherry Stevens was moving away from him. She had started a fresh bout of tears and was being comforted by Lisa Black. As I got nearer I saw her throw off Lisa Black's arm and walk off angrily.

"Is she upset about Louise?" I said to Lisa Black.

"Not exactly," Lisa said. "Boyfriend trouble. I said to her, boyfriends are more trouble than not."

But I wasn't listening to Lisa Black because further down the cemetery, across the heads of the mourners, I had just seen Joey Hooper come through the gates. Among all the white faces he stood out and I felt an urgent sense of alarm, like a silent fire bell that only I could hear.

"Sherry and Louise had the same taste in men. That's why they always quarrelled. I said to Sherry, you should go out with other people, then you and Lou wouldn't always be after the same guys."

I walked away from Lisa Black without a word. I could hear her complaining, *Don't mind me, just walk off why don't you.* But I wasn't concerned. I was concentrating, going slowly down the incline, keeping Joey Hooper in my sights. He had stopped for a moment and leant against an ornate gravestone. One or two of the mourners had noticed him and were pointing to him, probably wondering why he was there; a black face among a white crowd.

He should have been with his family. Now that Paul had died they needed him. I wanted to wave, to shout across the cemetery but it didn't seem the right thing to do. Why had he come? He hadn't known Louise; had only recognized her from the newspaper story. It only took a moment for me to find out.

Joey Hooper was only metres from Frank Ross when he put his hand into his pocket and pulled out the knife. I blinked a couple of times and then everything seemed to move in slow motion. The click of a switch and the blade was out. I could see it from that distance, glinting in the sunlight, and Joey's face wide in a smile of satisfaction. Frank Ross turned and saw what was waiting for him, his mouth dropping in shock. I was too far away to do anything, I couldn't even shout then because my vocal cords had turned to ice. Des Murray must have seen it to because I saw him move swiftly in the direction of Joey. Frank Ross started to back away, his mouth opening and closing. What he was saying, I couldn't hear. Joey was answering him and although I couldn't make out the words his voice came across the cemetery like a bugle.

I dodged past two, three, four people, losing sight of what was happening but getting closer, feeling the shocked stillness of the crowd and hearing a collective gasp and then people running and a lot of angry noise.

When I got to the front Des Murray had Joey Hooper in a hold. The other detective was radioing the station. Frank Ross was sitting on the ground, one hand on his arm. On the grass, next to a gravestone was the knife.

"You killed my brother, Ross! I'll never forget it and I'll never leave you alone!" Joey Hooper's words choked out through tears and rage.

"Joey," I said, quietly. He had found out that it was *Frank* who had beaten his brother up. Kevin Cooke must have told him.

Frank Ross struggled up, still holding on to his left

arm. There was blood bubbling up from between his fingers and he tightened his grip as though he thought his arm might fall off. He stuck his foot out and kicked the knife in the direction of Des Murray and Joey.

"Look what you've done to my suit, Hooper!" His voice was trembling and even though his mouth was twisted in a smile his eyes had a dazed and frightened look to them. "I want him charged for this! I want charges brought!" He coughed the words out.

Several people surrounded him quickly, a couple pulling him towards a car. Des Murray was shouting at them to wait for the ambulance, but in a few seconds he was in someone's back seat. The mourners moved back as the driver revved up, sending small stones everywhere, and then dramatically screeched out and towards the gate.

Joey Hooper was hanging limply in Des Murray's hold, staring dolefully at the knife that was on the ground. I went over to him. Several other people were mumbling in his direction, some older men who looked like they were working themselves up.

"Let's get him out of here, Patsy," Des said through clenched teeth.

I took Joey's other arm and led him towards the car while the other detective picked up the knife with a plastic bag. I could hear Des Murray saying, *You have the right to remain silent but I must…*

Once the car door clicked shut there was a soft silence. Outside we could see the mourners looking angrily at us but we couldn't hear their words.

"You're in big trouble, son," Des Murray said, brushing the dust off his jacket.

"I know," Joey said.

"Assault with a deadly weapon. Very bad. Very bad."

"You don't know the whole story," I said, sadly. Even the whole story wouldn't help Joey when he was in court, I knew that.

"What does it matter?" Joey said. "Nothing matters."

# 21
# Frank Ross

I'd been sitting for an hour and a half looking through videotapes in the police station. In front of me was a TV monitor and ten tapes, all from different parts of Oxford Circus underground station. I had to find the right section, approximately seven-fifty onwards, and slow the tape down so that I could look carefully at all the passers-by.

I concentrated hard, looking for the face of Frank Ross in a grey sweatshirt. In my mind a number of arrows were pointing directly at him. Frank Ross had been one of the kids who beat up Paul Hooper. He was also Louise's secret boyfriend. His brother Jack had tired of being blamed for the attack and had threatened to go to the police. This had put Louise into a panic because it may have meant her new lover being charged. So she'd gone to Lee Cooke. After the murder she'd told Frank what she had done. He'd been furious with her at the death of his brother. He was the one she had seen on the platform, not Kevin Cooke at all.

I was tense, hoping all the while that I wouldn't see Joey Hooper anywhere. Kevin Cooke had lied, I was sure, hoping to get Joey into trouble. He had no motive whatsoever for killing Louise.

Des Murray had been right about the grey sweatshirt being common. I was on to the fourth tape and I'd noted down four women and one older man wearing them. None of the faces looked familiar but there was always a slight chance that Louise had been pushed by some complete stranger for no particular reason at all.

Joey Hooper had been arrested, I knew. He'd refused to get in touch with his parents and was put in a holding cell while a duty solicitor was called for. I'd watched as they had taken him off, down the stairs, his body slouched, his face blank. I saw one of the uniformed officers raise his eyebrows at the "H" sculpted in his hair and I wanted to say something. I didn't, though.

Des Murray had gone to the hospital and picked up Frank Ross. He'd been sceptical about my theory but had agreed that there was enough to question him about.

He'd been congratulated by several people in the

station as soon as we'd got back from the funeral. The word had gone round that he'd prevented a killing by being quick and courageous. I was loath to join in, but I had to grudgingly admit that things might have been a lot worse, not only for Frank Ross but for Joey Hooper as well, if he had not stepped in. I saw a new side of Des Murray; his swagger and half-moon smile made him look a different man. I can't say I liked him any more.

I got a fresh video out and began to scan through it until I reached the right time. Then I let it run at normal speed, using the remote to stop it every few seconds and check on familiar faces or grey hooded sweatshirts.

The door opened behind me and Des Murray was there.

"Want to watch this interview with Frank Ross?" he said, graciously. Being a hero obviously made him generous. I turned the TV off, picked up my bag and followed him out.

I sat in an empty, darkened room and looked through a window into another brightly lit interview room. Between the two rooms was a window of smoked glass. It was called the "interview suite" as though we weren't in a police station but a hotel. I'd seen it many months before when I'd been shown round the station while on a case. The people in the interview room couldn't see through the glass, but I could see them clearly as though they were on a giant TV screen. In the middle, sitting at a table, was Frank Ross, his arm bandaged up and in a sling. Beside him was an older man in a suit. He had an attaché case balanced on his knee and a pad of A4 paper on it ready to take notes. I wondered if Frank had got a solicitor from the place where he worked.

They were talking quietly to each other. Behind them, on a chair, reading a newspaper, was a uniformed officer. A couple of seconds later Des Murray walked in and started to fiddle with the cassette recorder.

While he was doing it, I found myself staring straight at Frank Ross and the odd thing was that he seemed to be staring straight back at me. He worked in a solicitor's office so he probably knew that the interview was being watched, knew what the glass was there for. The unsettling thing was that he had his eyes focused on the direct spot where I was sitting, *as if he knew that I was there.* I found myself looking away from his stare and it was as if he could see because he gave a little smile and began to nod his head.

Des Murray began to talk, giving the time and the date of the interview. He stretched back in his chair and started to ask a question when the solicitor intervened. The man spoke with an accent that made me think of Horse Guards' Parade, Palace tea parties and fox hunting.

"My client wishes to assist the police in every way possible. He has informed me of all the factors involved in this case and admits that there are certain circumstances that have not been made public. My client is willing to make a clean breast of these circumstances, so as to bring about a speedy resolution to this whole sorry business."

"What business are we talking about?" Des Murray said gruffly.

"The death of Mr Jack Ross."

"What about the death of Paul Hooper or Louise Palmer?" Des Murray said sharply.

*Good for you!* I thought.

"My client has no comment to make on any other matter."

The solicitor closed his eyes and smiled sweetly. Then he sat back. Des Murray didn't look at all ruffled. He glared at Frank Ross.

"Thanks, Robert," Frank said and turned a nervous face to Des. "Louise Palmer was my brother's girlfriend. They'd been going out for about a year, I think. I actually didn't know her very well at first. Me and Jack didn't really socialize, not much. Although we were twins we kept pretty much to ourselves. Anyway, about three months ago I think it was, Jack asked me if I'd like to go and see one of Lou's dance performances at this place near Liverpool Street. I had nothing better to do so I went. It was the first time I'd ever really talked to

Lou and I liked her. She asked me to do her a favour; she asked me if I'd go out with her friend. The girl, Sherry, she was all right. We must have gone out, the four of us, about half a dozen times and then, I'm not quite sure exactly when, it stopped. The thing was, I did like this girl, but I was beginning to like Lou more. There was a real attraction between us. This particular night the four of us were supposed to meet to have a drink and go to the cinema. The arrangement must have been messed up because the other two turned up at the pictures and Lou and me, we met at the pub. We ended up staying there all evening and that was where it started."

Frank Ross had been involved with Sherry Stevens. Why hadn't anybody told me that?

"Me and Lou started to see each other on the quiet. Secret dates, meetings. I knew it would cause a big fuss if Jack found out. I kept thinking that it would end. I've never been that fond of any particular girl and I thought it wouldn't last."

"How can you be sure that Jack never knew?" Des Murray said.

I had another question in my head. Did Sherry Stevens ever know?

"He didn't know. He was single-minded, Jack was, full of himself. He never guessed at all. Lou wanted to split up with him but I knew it would be upsetting for everybody, my parents particularly. I s'pose the truth was I didn't really know how I felt about her, in the long run, I mean."

"What about after Jack was murdered? What happened then?"

Frank Ross looked at his solicitor, who gave a brief nod of his head.

"After Jack died Lou was in a terrible state. Eventually she told me that she had gone to Lee Cooke and told him that Jack had been threatening to go to the police about the incident at Highbury."

"She told him that Jack was going to grass the lot of you up about the attack on Paul Hooper?" Des Murray said, with a grin.

"My client has absolutely no comment to make." The solicitor gave another weedy smile and carried on making notes.

"She told me that she hadn't meant for anything really bad to happen. She'd just wanted Jack to be frightened off from going to the police. But it all went wrong. My parents were devastated. I couldn't stomach it. You won't believe it but she started to see it as a way for us to be together. I told her it was all over. I told her to get out of my life. And then she did. She disappeared. I never saw her alive again."

"What about the night she died? Did you go to Oxford Circus to meet her that night?" Des said.

"I told you, after she disappeared I never saw her alive again."

Frank Ross turned and looked at his solicitor. The man stopped writing and cleared his throat.

"I think I can help you with these details, Mr Murray. On the night of the murder Frank Ross was at a Law Society function at the Town Hall. I was there, so was my wife and several other company members. I honestly don't think he could have a better alibi than that."

Des Murray's shoulders dropped and he turned full circle and looked straight into the mirror at me. I held his eyes for a moment and felt the floor falling away beneath me.

Frank Ross hadn't been there that night. He had a cast-iron alibi.

Back in the video room I had a long cup of coffee. I put my feet up on the desk and let the swivel chair turn back and forth, rocking myself gently, going over it all in my head.

The one new thing that I had overheard in the interview suite was that Sherry Stevens and Frank Ross had gone out together. I let this play about in my head for a while, while the coffee burned its way down the back of my throat. In front of me the video was on *pause.* A frozen scene of people rushing about on the Underground.

Sherry Stevens had gone out with Frank Ross half a dozen times. Then Louise had secretly taken up with him. Had Sherry known, at the time?

I pressed the *play* button and let the video film run forward, keeping half an eye open for grey hooded sweatshirts. It was a tape I'd already looked at once.

I remembered Lisa Black describing Louise getting out of a car and being terrified that anyone should know. I remembered Louise's reported words: *Please don't tell a soul ... especially not Sherry.* And then, at the cemetery, there'd been some kind of row between Frank and Sherry. Sherry had been crying and Lisa Black had said, *Sherry and Louise had the same taste in men. That's why they always quarrelled.*

I paused the video again and looked for Ben Fryer's statement. I found it under a load of papers. He had said that the person who pushed Louise had been wearing a grey hooded sweatshirt with the hood up. He had called that person a "he". We had all assumed that it was a "he". I certainly had.

But what if it had been a *woman* who pushed Louise over, a woman in a grey sweatshirt?

I fast forwarded to the place on the tape that I was looking for. The time was 7:58 and I slowed the picture down and finally paused it. The woman's face was largely hidden by a young boy who was in front of her, being told off and smacked by his mother. The grey sweatshirt was clearly visible and the woman was young, but the hair that flicked out the side of her hood was blonde.

I let the picture run on a couple of seconds and the little boy moved out of the way. I had a full shot of the top half of the blonde woman's body. I paused it and looked closely at the picture. The face was big, framed with pale blonde hair. I clenched my fist in annoyance, thinking of Sherry's thick black hair.

Then I had what I can only describe as a mental nudge and I remembered watching another TV monitor some days before. I'd been standing in the foyer of Jingles. A number of girls in blonde wigs had danced across a stage. One of them had been Sherry Stevens, wearing her costume and rehearsing the musical *East Side Story.*

Sherry had worn the blonde wig underneath a hooded sweatshirt and gone to Oxford Circus. She had been somewhere behind me on the station and when Louise had looked and waved at me she had seen her old friend there. When the red balloon had floated into the air, Sherry had taken advantage of the diversion and crept through the crowds, catching up with Louise.

She killed her best friend for a boy she'd only been out with a half a dozen times. I shook my head in disbelief.

I picked up the tape and went to look for Des Murray. He was still involved in the interview, though, and couldn't be interrupted. I left the tape and a quickly scrawled note saying what I thought and where I would be. Then I phoned Billy on the mobile and left the station.

# 22
# East Side Story

The rehearsal for *East Side Story* had started and me and Billy slipped into the tiny theatre space and sat at the back watching it. There were about twenty dancers on the stage. Half of them were white, in blonde wigs, males and females. The other half were black dancers all wearing long beaded African hair-pieces. The contrast was striking, and the dancing was energetic and full of passion.

There were no words or singing, just backing music and a kind of silent version of *Romeo and Juliet*, set against a changing backdrop of photographs of local East End sights. I recognized the London Hospital, the Blind Beggar, Tower Bridge, Petticoat Lane Market, the Docklands and Cable Street. All the time the dancers were moving gently to and fro, telling their story with physical language.

Sherry Stevens was a chorus dancer and I watched as she kept time with the others, her facial expression changing from joy to sorrow, then back to laughter or anger. Her dancing was faultless and I felt impressed and amazed at the same time. How could such a strong, attractive girl, who seemed to have everything going for her, suddenly push her best friend under a tube train just for the sake of a boy she'd been out with a few times?

Pushing someone under a train. The end result was murder, but if you cut the act in half it didn't really seem like it. Using a knife or a gun or even a weapon to hit someone with, meant that you came into physical contact with their death. You caused their blood to spill, or you knocked the consciousness out of them. That really seemed like murder. But to *push* someone. It was an everyday act. It was a curiously non-violent way to kill someone, even though they ended up dead.

My thoughts were getting tangled up and I was glad when the dance finished and the dancers went off to the changing area. The lights went on as the director went around patting people on the back, looking pleased with himself. Sherry Stevens was smiling with pleasure until she noticed me. Her eyes caught mine for a moment and then I watched her disappear through the door of the changing rooms. A couple of minutes later, I saw a young dancer come out of the door and skip across the room towards me.

"Are you Patsy Kelly?" she said.

I nodded.

"Sherry says she'll meet you in the Studio Café in fifteen minutes."

And then she danced off.

"Are you sure she'll turn up?" Billy said, his forehead wrinkled up.

"Yep," I said. "She doesn't know why I'm here. Remember, she doesn't think much of me. She probably thinks I just want to ask her a few more questions."

The Studio Café was about a hundred metres along the road. It was a small, hot place, full of cigarette smoke and the smell of dark, strong coffee. As soon as we sat down Billy took a packet of twenty out and placed it in the middle of the table. I could see that there was only one cigarette left inside it.

"My last smoke," he said.

"You're giving them up?" I said, relieved.

"You want me to, don't you?"

"It's up to you. It's got to be your choice," I said. I meant it too. There was no point in trying to force someone to give something up if they didn't want to.

"I do want to," Billy said, frowning, giving the box a look of longing.

Just then my mobile phone rang. Several other people in the café started to feel for their phones as I answered mine. All the time I was looking out the window, impatient for Sherry to come along.

"Patricia. I've been trying to get hold of you. It's Tony."

"Hi, Tony," I said. My uncle Tony, the ruthless businessman who had thrown me out of a job. "How's the diet?" I said, lightly, as if I didn't bear the scars of redundancy.

"Three pounds on my home scales," he said. "Look, I got a couple of interesting letters and phone calls this morning. That big superstore down near the railway? You know it? By the garage? Well, they've written and asked for me to go round and view their security arrangements. As well as that, that big bookshop in the Exchange has asked for a visit. It seems that someone is coming into the shop and vandalizing their books!"

"Yeah?" I said, wondering what the point was.

"And on top of that a new insurance company, a small group that's recently started up, have asked me to look into some claims. These people have all come out of the woodwork. I've no idea how they got hold of my name."

"Really?" I said, thinking back to my creative letter-writing exercise when I was still in employment.

Then I saw Sherry Stevens walking along the road. She had the tan coat on that she'd had when I first followed her, the day that Louise was killed. It was flowing out behind her and she looked theatrical, as though she was making an entrance. She stopped at the kerb for a moment and let a motorcycle courier go by. Her lips were opened and I could see her teeth clenched behind them.

"It's just that I need you to come back," I could hear my uncle saying. "I'm desperate. I've got all this new business and no one to help me do it!"

"I can't talk right now," I said as Sherry Stevens came into the café.

"I'll give you a raise," he carried on.

"I really can't talk now. I'll call you later," I said and pressed the *cut* button.

Sherry Stevens saw me and walked across and sat herself down. She had the usual superior expression on her face and her body language was geometric, her shoulders and arms all right angles and stiff.

"Who's your friend, Patsy?"

I introduced Billy.

"What's happening?" she said. "I hear they've picked up Frank Ross. Surely he didn't have anything to do with Louise's death?" She gave me a quick smile.

It was then I realized that she was rattled. The smile gave it away. Her previous rudeness had gone. It was a sign that she was less sure of herself.

"Why didn't you tell me you'd been involved with Frank Ross?" I said.

"Frank Ross? That was months ago. What does it have to do with anything?"

"I've got evidence, Sherry, that you were on the platform when Louise died."

"You can't have!" she said, giving a forced laugh.

"You were wearing a blonde wig and a hooded top, but you were seen pushing Louise," I said, embroidering the truth a little.

"That's rubbish. Why would I want to push Louise? She was my best friend! Nope. You've got it wrong again, Patsy."

"She was your best friend until she told you that she and Frank Ross were lovers. Frank Ross, who you'd gone out with. Maybe you were in love with him."

"I didn't love Frank Ross, he was just a kid that Louise set me up to go out with. I knew she was going out with him. I've known for weeks. I didn't care."

"You were there, Sherry. We've got a videotape of you leaving the station. We've got evidence from a witness that she was pushed. You were jealous of her."

I felt Billy's foot kick me under the table and I looked to see that an unmarked police car had pulled up across the street and Des Murray had got out and was talking to another officer. Sherry Stevens didn't seem to notice. She seemed deep in thought.

"It was Louise who was in love with Frank Ross, not me," she said.

"We know that," I said quietly.

A change was coming over Sherry Stevens. Where she had previously been upright, all straight lines, now her shoulders and arms had rounded and she seemed to have sunk down into the chair.

"That was the thing about Louise. She thought about everything from her own point of view. She thought Jack was so madly in love with her that he wouldn't be able to exist if she left him. So she two-timed him. Then, when Jack got fed up with being blamed for the fight over at Highbury, she went and told Lee Cooke that he was going to go to the police. She was so afraid that her precious Frank would end up going to prison. She didn't understand Frank at all, though. Frank was as self-centred as she was. He was just having fun. He didn't really want Louise."

"But if you didn't love him, what reason did you have for hating Louise? For pushing her under the train?"

"I hated her because of Jack. It was Jack that I was in love with. And he was in love with me. He would have left Louise, in the end."

She looked straight at me. *Jack Ross and Sherry were lovers?*

"It started when we were all going out in four-somes. I didn't even *like* Frank Ross very much.

There was something underhand about him. Oh, he wore nice suits and talked about the solicitor's office he worked in, but there was something not quite *honest* about him. Jack, on the other hand, *was* honest. What you saw was what you got. One night I remember there was an arrangement for us all to go out. There was a mix-up. Louise and Frank had thought we were meeting at a pub, but Jack and I turned up at the cinema. We waited for them to come, missed the start of the film. We went for a walk and then a drink. Nothing happened, but I knew that we liked each other. A few days later, he came to Jingles to meet Louise but she wasn't there, so he and I had a coffee. In here it was."

She stopped speaking and looked around the tiny café.

"In this café. Over at that table, Jack on one side, me on the other. That's when it all started. I never thought that I could just fall for someone just like that. I tell you I was dizzy every time he left. It was like being on a fairground ride."

"But you knew about Louise and Frank, so why didn't you tell Jack?" Billy said. "Surely that was the easy way to resolve it all. He would have left her then."

"It didn't seem right. I wanted him to leave her for me, not because she was two-timing him with his brother." Her mouth was pinched up. "When Louise came and stayed with me, I believed what she told me.

I thought that Jack had been killed in some terrible, freak stabbing. She was upset, she cried a lot. I didn't even mind that. I thought that even though she'd been seeing Frank behind Jack's back she was probably still upset about his death. Anybody would be. I accepted her story. I didn't tell her that I knew about her and Frank. What was the point? It wasn't going to bring Jack back, what did it matter?" She looked at me for a moment. "After you came and Louise had been at Lisa's we met here, late in the afternoon."

"She told you about Jack's death," I said.

"I believe she was actually feeling *guilty*. She said she'd told Lee Cooke that Jack was going to go to the police and inform on him. She said she'd thought that Lee would just frighten Jack into keeping his mouth shut. It all went wrong, though, and Jack ended up dead. I've never felt such pure hatred for anyone in my life."

"And so you decided to kill her."

Her eyes had a far-away look, as if she were remembering. A tiny smile formed on her lips. Outside, Des Murray had seen us and was moving from foot to foot with impatience. I thought he would probably come in at any minute.

"Honestly, Patsy," she finally said, her voice taking on some of its former cockiness, "you should have been there. It was just a little push," she held the flat of her hand up on the table and moved it towards me, "just a tiny little push."

The train driver came into my head, crying out with grief, stumbling up the platform, the crowds opening up to let him through. He would never forget it, I knew. Somewhere, beneath the pulsating mass of the train, Louise Palmer lay like a broken doll.

Billy had lit up his last ever cigarette and I saw Des Murray pushing open the door of the café.

"I *was* there, Sherry," I said. "That's the whole point. I was there."

# 23

## Justice

Sherry Stevens made a statement at the station. Des Murray had said that she was as cool as cucumber. *She'll be out in ten years*, he'd said, derisively, *nice-looking girl like that. She's still got her life ahead of her.* Unlike Louise Palmer, I'd thought at the time.

After the court hearing it came out in the local paper. The headline was DANCER ARRESTED IN LOVE TRIANGLE MURDER. Inside, there were pictures of the girls in different dancing costumes and a lot of comments from Lisa Black, who, apparently, had known all along that Sherry Stevens was a violent and unstable person. She was said to be still *devastated* over the loss of her close friend, Louise Palmer.

Further down the page was a column with the headline, KNIFE ATTACK AT FUNERAL. Underneath it described the stabbing and put it down to gang rivalry suggesting a possible *race motive.* There was no mention of Paul Hooper or his death in the article.

Joey Hooper was sent on remand. Des Murray said that he'd seemed over-confident in court, looking everyone straight in the eye, with no hint of remorse. It wasn't hard to imagine. I wondered whether the court would take his background into consideration, the fact that his brother had been half killed in an attack and that for six months Joey had spent some part of every single day at his bedside. How many men would have kept that up?

I suppose someone must have noted it, because they let him out for his brother's funeral. Me and Billy didn't go. Even though we'd been involved with Joey over the past couple of weeks, we didn't want to intrude on an occasion that should have been just close family and friends.

Perry went to the funeral. He came along to Billy's house later in the afternoon. He was wearing a suit and looked entirely different, like a bank clerk. He was subdued and quiet and I made him a cup of tea. He said that Joey Hooper had arrived at the church under police escort. He'd stayed for the service and then went along to the cemetery. After the prayers and sermons were over, he'd been taken back into custody, even though his mother and father had pleaded with the officers to let him stay a little longer.

Perry said he'd been nervous all the way to the church because he thought the Cooke brothers might be hanging round somewhere along the way. I hadn't even known they'd let Lee Cooke out. Once Louise's death appeared to have no link with him or his brother, the case against him for Jack Ross's stabbing must have collapsed.

I saw Heather Warren, the detective inspector, a few days later and asked her about it. She'd been just going into a meeting and couldn't talk for long.

"Apart from Louise Palmer there was no other evidence against Lee Cooke. Once the truth came out that she was involved in Jack Ross's death her statement couldn't be relied on. There was just no case against him. His barrister would have got it thrown out of court."

"What about Joey Hooper?" I said.

"There's dozens of witnesses from the funeral. There's the knife with his fingerprints and Frank Ross's blood. Joey Hooper will be found guilty. I'm sorry, Patsy, but that's the way the law works. We have to have evidence."

"What about justice?" I said.

She didn't answer. She stuck her pen in the side of her mouth and pointed to her watch, then went off to her meeting.

Paul Hooper was dead and his brother was on remand, awaiting trial for a serious assault charge which would almost certainly result in him being sent to prison. Lee and Kevin Cooke were free to roam the streets. Frank Ross was still working in the solicitor's, a promising career in front of him.

It wasn't right and it wasn't my idea of justice.

The day after the funeral, Billy and I went to the car auctions. Billy had put Perry off so that we could go on our own. It was a fiercely cold day, and I found myself longing for some of the warm rain that had been drenching us all for the previous few weeks. After a while my fingers were so numb that I began to blow hot air on to them. Billy, seeing my efforts to warm up, took my hand and put it, with his, into his jacket pocket. From time to time he curled and uncurled his fingers, tickling my hand and making me shiver and smile at the same time.

We walked along, looking at row upon row of cars, arguing about which was the best one to buy. In the end he kept looking at an old black Ford Escort that had been squashed up like an accordion.

"You won't be able to repair that," I said, dismissively.

"Please, Patsy. Are you talking to me?"

"It's beyond repair."

"Not to me," he said. "You look after your own work and I'll look after mine."

"I see. So you're never going to give me any advice again on crime detection?"

"I only offer advice when it's asked for," he said, laughing.

"It's a wreck," I said, shaking my head. "You definitely shouldn't buy it. Take my advice."

But he didn't. He paid for the car and we walked towards the exit. I pulled my hat further down on my head to keep the cold from gripping on to my ear lobes.

"You going back to work tomorrow?" He put his arm lightly around my shoulder.

"Yep. You should hear my uncle Tony. According to him I'm the best thing that's ever happened to his agency, and guess what? I'm getting a raise!"

"You can afford to take *me* out then!"

"Hey," I pushed him away. "I always pay my way!"

"A decent Christmas present at the very least," he said.

"Aren't you being presumptuous? What makes you think I'll still be going out with you at Christmas?"

He frowned at this, his forehead wrinkling up and for a moment my spirits took a dive and I thought I'd gone too far, been too cheeky, spoilt the moment.

"You and me, Patsy," hugging my shoulders, "I got this feeling. We're always going to be together."

*You and me together always.*

It was a cliché, I knew. I smiled anyway. A silly, first-time-in-love smile, and we walked on down the road.